EROTIC ROMANCE

Almost
BROKEN
HEALED COMPLETELY!

KERRY JAMES

WARNING

This book contains sexually explicit scenes and adult language. It may be considered offensive to some readers. This book is for sale to adults ONLY.

* * * * * * * * * * * * * * * * * * *

Please store your files wisely where they cannot be accessed by underage readers.

Please feel free to send me an email. Just know that these emails are filtered by my publisher. Good news is always welcome.

Kerry James - **kerry_james@awesomeauthors.org**

About the Publisher

4Fun Publishing, a member of **BLVNP Incorporated**, 340 S. Lemon #6200, Walnut CA 91789, info@blvnp.com / legal@blvnp.com

NOTE: Due to the highly emotional reaction of some people to works of erotic fiction, any email sent to the above address that contains foul language or religious references is automatically deleted by our anti-spam software and will not be seen. All other communications are welcome.

DISCLAIMER

Please don't be stupid and kill yourself. This book is a work of FICTION. Do not try any new sexual practice that you find in this book. It is fiction and not to be confused with reality. Neither the author nor the publisher or its associates assume any responsibility for any loss, injury, death or legal consequences resulting from acting on the contents in this book. Every character in this book is over 18 years of age. The author's opinions are not to be construed as the opinions of the publisher. The material in this book is for entertainment purposes ONLY. Enjoy.

Almost Broken

Healed Completely!
Erotic Romance

By: Kerry James

© **Kerry James 2014**
ISBN: 978-1-68030-154-0

CHAPTER ONE

Where does life take us? Why is it that when you have settled on one course, fate comes knocking at your door and takes you off on a tangent? That's what happened to me, it seems to keep happening to me. I get used to my life, and then fate throws a surprise my way. Sometimes it is a little tap-tap on the door, at others it's a loud knock. Sometimes it blows the door open, and when it is really serious fate just takes the thing off with its hinges.

I am Jack Hunter. My life to date had been particularly uneventful, although that would depend on your point of view. I had a wife, and a daughter. I also had an affair which while it didn't become the reason for my divorce, soured me sufficiently to seek to split with my wife. I will hold my hand up and acknowledge that I cheated on my wife. Not a good thing to do, but I will say in my defence that because my wife was in love with the bottle; Vodka and Tonic was her favourite so no one could be actually sure whether she was tippling or not. Our love life was virtually zero. It's no easy task to make love to someone who reeks of alcohol. Brenda, my wife didn't appear to be bothered by our lack of intimacy, her next drink was far more important. I tried to get her to admit the problem, her Doctor tried, her mother tried, even our daughter, Libby, only three years old but she understood that something was wrong with mummy. Nothing worked. Despair and frustration were taking my self-esteem to new depths so when I had met a rather lovely lady called Deborah it quickly went from acquaintance to friendship to lovers. Our affair went on for three years. But when I called quits on my marriage, and as you would expect got taken to the cleaners in the resulting divorce, Deborah made it plain that we were not going to be an item. She came round for the sex but nothing else. Sounds like any man's dream, doesn't it? I had sex on tap and no emotional baggage to go with it. But I was one of those men who wanted emotion in a relationship, so eventually I told her it was over.

The legal process in the UK was slow but exacting. It had however problems in making its judgments effective. I had visiting rights with my daughter, which were denied or delayed for spurious reasons. My solicitor would petition the court again and again to enforce the judgment. The court would confirm the judgment but never took action to ensure it was complied with. So slowly I lost touch with my daughter.

I met Jasmine in a supermarket; I actually helped her with the heavy bags. We had coffee, then dinner and eventually we started sleeping together on occasional nights. We went on like this for five years, until one day I got a fixed penalty speeding fine in the post. The location was not one I had driven through for months, so I queried the penalty. The bloody camera was right, it was my car, but at the time I had been away at a trade show, and I had travelled to the show by train. There was only one person who had access to my house, and the keys to the company car. Jasmine! After a lot of heated arguments she admitted she had 'borrowed' the car. Problem was that she was not insured to drive it, a criminal offence in the UK. If she admitted the offence to the police, chances were that she would certainly be banned from driving, and get a hefty fine. There was also an outside chance of a prison sentence. I paid the fine, took the points on my licence, and Jasmine became history.

A few months after that lesson, I was invited to a party at a friend's house, which was where I met Bridget. We were under no illusions that we had been invited by well-meaning friends who thought that being single was an offence against nature. Well we did hit it off. Remaining friends for nearly ten years, but the tingle was just not there. She was looking for a life-time partner. So was I really, but we knew that we were not the person who could fill that role for each other. The friendship continued for a while until Bridget found the right man for her. We made the usual comments; you know the ones about remaining friends and seeing each other from time to time. We all know that is just hot air. We would talk on the phone occasionally, but even that faded away. So I was again a single man at forty-nine. Probably, I thought for the rest of my life, judging from my track record. Perhaps I should have tried harder with my wife, but regrets are something we have to live with. You can't go back in time and correct your mistakes, although often you wish you could.

I worked as a salesman for a textile wholesaler. I had never considered myself a great salesman, but I made up for that with a sound knowledge of fabric technology and also how fabrics were woven printed and used. I had literally gone through the mill, the real dark satanic mills. That was when the U.K. still produced textiles. Most of the stuff we sold was to bespoke curtain suppliers, and at one time I had my own business making curtains, I could cut the cloth, do the sewing and make up a good pair of curtains. My business was another casualty of my divorce. That talent though, served me well when talking to Interior Designers who mostly had absolutely no idea how to make the designs they created.

My area was quite large stretching from the North Sea coast of Lincolnshire, to the Irish Sea of North Wales, so I had to stay away regularly. Lincolnshire was a county of contrast, the flat lands of the Fens in the south and the rolling hills of the Wolds in the north. It was quite eerie driving the long straight roads back to my hotel over the Fens of a November evening. The gathering gloom cast a strange purple-grey miasma over the unending flat fields, only the solitary lights of a farmhouse away in the distance could convince you that there was at least some life here. The morning drive could be amazing. The roads were laid on embankments, as all the land was below sea level. When the temperatures were right a mist would cover all the fields, lapping gently at the road on its embankment. It was like driving on top of a cloud, fantastic! North Wales was a complete contrast, the mountains and sea pushed timelessly at each other, leaving just a thin strip of land upon which the seaside towns, the road and the railway had established themselves. There were a lot of Welsh-speakers there, who viewed the English with caution if not dislike. It took me many visits to gain their confidence. I did one thing that pleased them. I learned how the place names were pronounced, asking them if I was getting it right. They seemed to warm to me as I was at least trying.

We often got requests from new businesses wanting to establish account facilities with us, and one such request was from Rebecca Cannon. She was working from home in a town not too far from where I lived so I phoned and made an appointment to call and see her. It was usual with new accounts to show as much of the range as possible, so my car, a Ford Mondeo was loaded to the gunwales with pattern books, all of which I carried in for her to make selections and they were heavy. No need to go to the gym, weight lifting came with the job. I had explained to her that it would take some time to go through the range and to allow at least two hours. She was good and didn't hurry me so I got to know her quite well, particularly as she provided good coffee. Becky, as she preferred to be called took a good selection of the range and we discussed the terms. I filled in the application and we were up and running. She was a very pleasant woman, friendly with a rather earthy sense of humour; she was pretty, but well built. Her husband's name was Tom and he worked shifts, so he was there for some of the time. I got on well with him, although I did detect some acidity in things they said to each other. Not my problem, I did my job and eventually took off to my next call.

For the next couple years I would see Becky about four times a year. Two of the calls were to show her new ranges and the other calls were purely customer courtesy calls. Over this time we became quite good friends and the call time became longer, and more frequent. With the business over we would sit and chat. I learned quite a lot about her, and she about me. Again over that time I noticed that Becky who had been a well rounded girl was losing weight. I mentioned this and she told me that she had started going to the Gym, and had taken up riding again. I knew from previous conversations that she had once rode frequently, going to gymkhanas and even taking part in national trials. As she once said to me. "Riding a horse is not just about sitting on top of it. You work all the muscles and you sweat, almost as much as the horse. When you dismount your legs seem like rubber." I also gathered that she and Tom were not getting along too well. Now coming on to customers is not a sensible thing to do. So I never, ever gave Becky any reason to think that I was interested in her sexually, a fact she noticed. As she had lost weight, the great figure that had been hidden for years re-emerged, and she got come-ons from quite a few men. She mentioned this one day, and then went on to say. "That's why I like you, Jack. I think we are good friends, and one reason for that is that you have never done or said anything that could be suggestive. I don't have to be on my guard with you, and that's great. We can just talk about anything." Which we did.

Now don't get the idea that I didn't find Becky attractive. She was. However as I said she was a customer, and secondly married. I knew the marriage was shaky, but that is absolutely the worst time to make moves on a woman. So our friendly customer relationship went on. My calls with her got longer and I learned more about her background.

The relationship changed when on one call I told Becky of my determination to learn how to Ballroom Dance. I was one of those who got bitten by the bug after the first season of 'Strictly come Dancing', the programme is called 'Dancing with the Stars' in the States. All those gorgeous girls set the pulse racing. She asked me if I had a partner. "No. But the bloke who runs the classes said that there were plenty of single women there, and getting a partner would be no trouble, he said I may get killed in the rush!"

Becky laughed. Then floored me. "Jack, would you consider me to partner you?"

I was stuck for a reply for a while. "Well I would be happy, but what about Tom. Wouldn't he mind?"

Becky shook her head. "No, not at all, but let's ask him. He's in his workshop out the back." Becky went out. Then called from the kitchen. "Do you want another coffee while I'm here?"

"Thanks, Becky."

Five minutes later, Tom came in. "Hello Mate." He clapped me on the shoulder. "Becky told me about your going to dancing lessons, and that you're worried that I would be iffy about her going with you. No, mate. No trouble. Get her out a bit more. It'll be good for her." I did get the idea that it could be good for him as well.

We discussed what evenings would be best. Tom had gone back to his workshop by then, and it did strike me oddly that Becky didn't want to go to the classes nearest to her. They were only three miles away and I thought would be convenient, but Becky insisted that the evenings they held the classes would not be right for her, so we arranged to go to the school about fifteen miles away. It was no problem to me as I lived closer to the second school. We left it like that, and I arranged for us to join on the next date they started a beginner's class. That was three weeks away.

Becky drove to my house that first evening of dance, and we went on together. I must say the lessons were a lot of fun. I had been concerned that I could be the oldest there and was re-assured when quite a few couples were older. Now we didn't exactly start twirling around the floor that first evening, in fact there was no music to dance to until right at the end. The Instructors were more concerned with us learning the basic Waltz steps with one variation, the Spin Turn. When we got back to my place, Becky accepted the offer of coffee, and we sat and chatted for a least an hour, before she decided that she should go home.

Subsequently Becky would make her own way to the class and I would meet her there. We seemed to be compatible when dancing, although once or twice she tried to lead. I had to repeat to her what the instructor had said. "In the Ballroom dance, the man leads and the woman should follow his lead." Now Becky was an independent woman, but she did subdue her natural instinct and allowed me to lead. After a few weeks of classes we were getting reasonably proficient, having gained a good knowledge of the steps in Waltz, Quickstep and Foxtrot. In addition we were able to get around the floor without falling over our own feet. It was good to hold Becky close at times, particularly in the quick turns, when in order to do them I had to hold her quite tightly. Her weight loss had revealed a very impressive bust. I told her on one of the first occasions that I had to hold her body against me. "I am going to hold you tight now. I shan't enjoy it, but it has to be done for the dance."

Becky laughed. "Of course you won't enjoy it." She then proceeded to press herself against me even harder than needed for the dance.

It was about this time that I noticed something odd. When the class was finished we said goodbye and Becky would give me a kiss on the cheek. I had always driven out of the car park first, as Becky seemed to take an age getting sorted. One thing I did note was that the first thing she would do upon getting back into her car was switch on her mobile phone. She had one of those with a flip top and quite a bright illumination. She never made a call, just looked at the screen. I got the impression she could have been reading a text message. Usually we would take different roads home, but one time I went a different way, coincidentally it was the road that Becky would use. Again I had been out of the car park before her; she never seemed in a hurry to get going. I was travelling north, doing about seventy, when suddenly she passed me like I was standing still. My thought was that she must have an emergency at home. That is until I asked her the next week if there had been a problem.

"No, Jack. Why would you think that?" I decided not to pursue this and took her through a new step we had been taught the last week. But my mind was wondering.

A week or two later, Becky made a strange request, that if Tom phoned when I got home, not to answer. OK I could do that as her home number was in the memory, and I had caller ID. It was that request that convinced me of something that I had suspected. Becky was seeing another bloke, and using our dancing lessons as a cover. I was not jealous, but I was upset that she should use me this way. On my next business call I tackled her, making certain that Tom was on shift first. "You are seeing someone, aren't you?" Becky had that guilty look on her face that told the truth whatever she said.

"Yes. I'm sorry."

"Becky you don't have to say sorry to me, I just wished that as your friend you could have told me earlier. I thought you just wanted to learn to dance; now it appears that you are using that as an excuse to get out of the house."

"I shouldn't have used you like that, Jack." She was contrite. "When you said you were going to dancing lessons, I jumped at the chance. Tom knows you and wouldn't have a problem, although he thinks the lessons go on much later than they actually do. If it's any consolation, I am enjoying the lessons immensely." It did alleviate my upset a little.

"Becky. I realise that you and Tom were not getting on too well. Is it getting close to break-up time?" Becky nodded unhappily.

"I think it is."

"Well I'm sorry about that, but under the circumstances I think we should call it a day on the dancing lessons."

"Why, Jack?"

"If you and Tom break up, I don't want my name mentioned as a probable reason, and Tom could think that a possibility. If he did and complained to my employers, I could be out of a job."

She was shocked. She hadn't thought it through. "I am sure he wouldn't do that."

"Can you guarantee that?" The pause was long enough to convince me that she couldn't. "Sorry, Becky, but I can't take the chance."

I was a little pissed off about this. First it had spoiled a friendship, second a good customer relationship, and thirdly I didn't have a partner for dancing. This far into the class schedule it would be difficult to pick up with another partner. You are supposed to be able to dance with any partner, once you know how to dance. But in the learning stages it is better to be at the same stage as your partner in the process.

My calls now did not have the frequency as before. We were still friendly, but the topics we could talk about were censored. The business she did with us dropped severely. I tried to find out from my competitors if they were picking up business from her. It's a strange thing in this trade, that although we all competed for business, you got to know your colleagues of the competition, quite well, and would often pass on information to each other over a friendly coffee. Becky wasn't pushing her business to others, so I assumed that she wasn't doing as well now. The consensus opinion amongst my competitors was that she wasn't actively seeking for work now.

Two years after we had that conversation my life changed. For years I had held some National Savings and Investment Premium Bonds. These went into a draw every month for a top prize of a million quid. I had never had any luck. Then I got the letter. No, it wasn't the top prize but it was significant. Half a million! With that money invested sensibly, and taking my pension early, I would be slightly better off than if I continued working. I didn't have to think long. I enjoyed working, but not to the extent that I would continue if I didn't have to. I put my notice in to my employers, and became an official lay about in the UK.

CHAPTER TWO

A few months later, I was enjoying my new life. Not at first I have to say. The old routine of getting out of bed at six-thirty in the morning, showering, shaving and getting ready for a day's work was hard to break, and being honest I was quite depressed for a month or so. What we do, defines us as people, and I no longer had that definition. I adapted though, I started writing the novel that I had been thinking about for years. I decided on a complete makeover of my garden. I enjoy a garden, but I'm not too happy about working in one in all weathers. So I designed a minimum maintenance plot that meant that I wouldn't need to spend hours keeping it tidy, weather notwithstanding, but I could go out and enjoy it when the weather was good. And I took to having at least three or four days away every other month. In my job I had travelled widely in the UK, but always passing through places on the way to another appointment. Now I could stop and look at the places I had previously passed through. What is the saying? Stop and smell the Grass! I stopped, smelt the grass, and the coffee.

I re-joined the dance classes at the next beginners' class, and found a partner there. She was a nice widowed lady called Elli. She was six inches shorter than me, and when she put on her dancing shoes with the three inch heel she came to just the right height. Her figure was slim with just the right amount of curves. Elli was another one bitten by the bug of 'Strictly come Dancing', and we danced together quite well. We would chat after the class, and she revealed a rather irreverent, quirky sense of humour. Over the weeks we did see each other outside of the classes, morning coffee, a couple of lunches, and one evening Dinner at a good Italian restaurant. But I realised, when we got to the kissing stage that although we got on well there was no spark. She realised that also. "Jack, on all accounts you are a good catch. You look good, you take care of yourself and you are reasonably well off. Some women would jump at you and ignore the fact that the spark between you and her isn't there. They would just accept that they have security for life. I am not one of those women. I like you, but there isn't that buzz that tells me to get my knickers off and do rude things with you, and for me there has to be that buzz. I had that with my husband, and we did things together which couldn't be printed in any newspaper I can tell you. So if you have no objection, let's continue dancing together and not try and turn this into something it will never be." I understood that and agreed, although the devil in me would have liked to know more about what she got up to with her husband. However she did tell me about a couple of other ladies at the class, who it seemed would be quite happy to accommodate me in any position. She was right about them too!

One of my ex-colleagues, Brian, called me one day. He had taken over part of my area. He told me that he had tried to contact Becky to show her some new ranges, and had spoken to her husband. "Well, her ex-husband, Jack. Did you know that she was playing around?"

"Well I had inkling, Brian." I wasn't going to give him the story, it would take too long. We chatted about things for a while, and then he had to get to an appointment. I sat back thinking about his news. I have to say I was not surprised she was now divorced. I hoped that she had found what she was looking for. I knew from experience that looking for the rainbow was usually futile.

Time goes past quite quickly when you are enjoying what you do and my writing was going well. The novel was about a young lady who was searching for her roots. It was set in the West Country, and involved a railway that had been closed years before. I had been told that if you want to write, write about something you know. Well I knew the West Country, and I knew about the old railways. I understood that I had set myself a challenge, telling the story from a woman's point of view. It was in some way a Rites of Passage novel as well. Would it ever be published? I doubt it, but that wasn't the ambition. I was writing for myself, for the sheer pleasure of putting this story; that had been in my mind for years down on paper. To alleviate the periodic spells of writer's block, I started writing short stories as well, the problem was that they then took over and it was the novel which went on the back burner. It got to the point where I hated being interrupted, so I was not best pleased one day when the phone rang. It was Becky!

I didn't recognise the number as it was a mobile number. I picked up the phone and said.

"Hello?"

"Jack. It's Becky." Her voice sounded tentative, as if she wasn't sure of the reception she would get.

"Hi, Becky. How are you these days?"

"I'm fine, Jack. But more important, how are you? I hear that you have retired."

"Yeah. Official lay about now. What's happening with you?"

"I've got this job now with an Estate Agent. It's going well."

"I'm pleased to hear that. I know that you and Tom are divorced, are you with that chap you were seeing?"

"I would have shit for brains if I were. No, Jack he was only in it as long as he was getting me into bed for quickies. As soon as my marriage blew up you couldn't see him for dust."

"I'm sorry to hear that Becky. You deserved better."

"Only someone as nice as you Jack would say that. You deserved to be treated better than I did. Jack I'm sorry about all of that. I lost a good friend."

"Water under the bridge, Becky."

"Jack! Can I come and see you?"

"Yes, of course. When would be convenient?"

"I'm sitting in my car about half a mile from you. Would now be an imposition?"

"Come right round. I'll put the coffee on."

"Jack, you're a star. See you in five." And so Becky walked back into my life.

I opened the door for her and she came in looking better than I had ever seen her. The weight loss had done her good. Her hair had highlights I hadn't seen before, and she was wearing a blouse with waistcoat over that, and a pair of black leather trousers that looked moulded to her thighs and legs. She gave me a wide smile and kissed me on the cheek. "It's great to see you again."

"Becky it's good to see you, but if I don't say anything for a minute, it's because I am trying to get over how good you look." If the smile could have gotten wider it would have.

"Thank you, Jack. An old girl like me needs a little encouragement now and again." Old girl? She couldn't be more than forty four I reckoned. We walked into the lounge and I suggested she sit down.

"That's if you can in those trousers." She laughed.

"I can sit down in them, Jack. It's getting them off that's the problem." Now I was not sure if that was innuendo or not. I decided to treat it as not.

"Still take your coffee the same way?" I asked. "Black with cold water added?" She looked at me in surprise.

"You remembered?"

"Becky I don't have all that many gorgeous women in my life. Of course I remember." I made the coffee, and I could hear Becky wandering about. Woman do that, they look at your furnishings and the ornaments, as if they can discern your character from them. I brought the coffee in.

"You've changed things here."

"Yes. When I retired I decided on quite a few changes, so I had the whole of the house done, and some new curtains. I had to get them whilst my credit was still there with the old company you know."

"It looks good. I would have done it for you, you know." I shrugged my shoulders.

"That may have been difficult for us both." She nodded.

"Yes, you're probably right. Why did you retire? You're nowhere near sixty five."

"Well I worked things out, and reckoned I could manage well enough on my investments and decided that there was more to life than working." I didn't say anything about the Premium Bond win. She nodded agreeing with me. She took a deep breath. I thought for a moment that the waistcoat would pop a button. She did have a very generous bust.

"I wanted to say I'm sorry, Jack." I was about to say it didn't matter when she went on. "I know what you were going to say, but it does matter. I was being a silly bitch at the time. I hurt Tom badly, and I involved you in something without your agreement. I never thought it through and I shudder now to think that you could have lost your job because of my selfish actions. No wonder my life became shit, just so I could have some excitement in my life. If I had any sense I should have chosen you to be my lover." I was temporarily struck dumb. Becky looked at me and started to laugh. "Don't be surprised, Jack. It could have been you know if it wasn't for the fact that I was your customer. I knew enough about you to know that you wouldn't have gone down that route."

"Well thanks for thinking of me that way." Becky had that look on her face. I knew the next question would be difficult.

"Didn't you ever think of me that way?"

"Yes, but I liked our friendship, it meant a lot. Experience tells me that making a lover out of a friend tends to lose both lover and friend."

Becky nodded in agreement. "Are you still dancing, Jack?"

"I go every week, yes."

"You must be good by now."

I laughed. "No, Becky. I can get round the floor without too many mistakes, but that's about it."

"I don't believe you. You seemed to pick up the steps so quickly."

"At first there aren't too many steps to learn; now they are throwing new steps at us every week. They are also insisting that we do the Samba, Rumba, and the Ballroom Jive. That was too much for me. My brain has gone to mush now, can't keep it all in my head."

"Oh, so you wouldn't want to dance with me once more."

I shook my head, believing that she wanted to go back to dancing classes. "Well actually I was thinking of stopping going to the classes."

"No, Jack. Not classes. I need a partner for a Ball I have to go to. It's work related, Dinner, speeches and dancing to a live band. It will be very posh. It will be long Frocks and Dinner jackets. It would be nice to be able to get round the floor with someone who knows what they're doing. It would be my treat."

"Come on Becky. You must have plenty of guys you could ask."

"Possibly, but none that know how to behave in that situation, and certainly none that could waltz me round the floor, and I know you can certainly do that."

That deserved some thought. The idea of going to a proper dance with a band had haunted me for some time. It was great to go and learn how to dance, but there was nowhere nowadays to actually go and dance. The ballrooms had either been turned into Bingo Clubs, or demolished in order that offices or housing should be built. Anywhere else there was live music, it was modern, Rap, Garage, not my cup of tea, nor suitable for a couple to do any kind of ballroom dance. Then again there was the chance to admire Becky in a long gown; I would imagine she would look fabulous. But! That little word loomed big in my mind. There was still a little hurt about how she had used me. OK I had inferred that it didn't matter. At the same time I had to consider that Becky may be trying to use me again. Forewarned is forearmed I decided. I would go, but keep my senses alive for any hint of duplicity. "When is this dance, Becky?"

"It's in two weeks time, Friday the twenty-second. Please say yes, Jack."

"OK. I shall look forward to it."

Becky was very happy. "Oh thanks. We should have a good evening."

We chatted on the phone a couple of times, making arrangements. I insisted that I would pick Becky up. I was not really a drinking man; once you have seen the damage alcohol makes to a person you stay away mostly. Going without alcohol apart from a glass of wine, would be no problem for me, whereas I knew that Becky liked to have a drink. She had given me her address, and I told her I would be there by seven for her. I looked the address up on the internet, and was a little surprised. I knew the town where she lived, and her address was not a good area at all. Having no use for one for years I had to hire a Dinner Jacket and I picked that up on the Friday.

I got to her just before seven and Becky was ready. I could see she had a long dress on, but couldn't tell what it was like as she wore a coat as well. When we came out I headed towards the silver Mercedes. Becky was confused until I flipped the remote and the lights flashed.

"Bloody Hell, Jack, a Merc?"

"Yes."

"Well I am glad I was ready. If you leave that sort of car around here for longer than ten minutes, the wheels would be gone. Leave it longer and the whole car would have gone!" I held the door for her as she got in.

"I always knew you were a gentleman, Jack. Thank you."

The venue was a Country Club about seven miles away. Becky left her coat at the cloak-room. She was a vision! She wore a lovely dress in Celadon Green that worked perfectly with her Dark brown hair. The front was cut into a low 'V' displaying her cleavage which was enhanced by her bra which pushed up and together. She was overwhelming but I have to say that for the most part the Ball was underwhelming. The food was edible, but catering for four hundred people who all sat down at the same time was going to challenge most kitchens. The speeches after were the usual self congratulating, and grovelling stuff. Perhaps if I had known the people it may have been better. There was a hiatus after the meal, as all the tables had to be re-arranged to clear the floor for dancing. People held drinks and mingled and chatted whilst this happened. Becky was in her element, she introduced me as her friend holding onto my arm tightly as if to suggest that there was more than friendship there. I chatted with many of those to whom I had been introduced. Once a salesman, always a salesman, you never get out of the habit. However Becky was quite particular in whom she talked to. The light flashed on in my head. She was networking! Becky was looking for another job. Giving the impression that she was in stable relationship may help. I was being used again. I quickly sussed who was the target. His name was Richard Ewing. I knew of his business, one of the largest Estate Agencies in the whole county, with links to a nationwide organisation. He dealt, not just in residential, but commercial and industrial as well. Oh well Becky had targeted the right man.

I got to chat with Richard as well. He was polite but cold. I doubted that I would have liked him, getting this undercurrent from him that he viewed people as commodities, use and throw away. He had obviously decided that I was of little use to him and could be ignored. I thought I would have to warn Becky, she was angling for the big fish, and may find she had caught a Shark.

At long last the floor was clear and the band started to play. We found a table and brought our drinks over. I was on sparkling water; Becky was drinking Vodka and Coke. There were few couples who dared to dance at first, so I said to Becky. "It would look good for you if you were amongst the first to dance. Shall we?" The look I got could have been apprehension about dancing, or it could have been that she realised that I had discovered her purpose. However my telling her that it would look good for her firmed up her mind. She nodded.

"Yes, let's."

As we took our position I muttered. "Remember, you follow, I lead." She grinned, and we went into hold. It may have been three years, but she hadn't forgotten the first thing we were taught. Her left hand rested lightly on my right upper arm, and her head turned away slightly. It was the perfect frame for ballroom dancing. Thankfully it was a Waltz, just about the easiest of the repertoire of ballroom dance, and she did follow me, even through the Spin turn and through the Whisk.

"Well done." I whispered.

"Don't get any more complicated than that for the moment, please Jack." The floor was filling up now so there was little chance of doing anything flashy.

After we got back to our table Becky was delighted with herself. "Jack that was great. I had thought I would struggle, yet when you went through those steps I followed you and it was easy. You are a good dancer you know."

"Shall we try the Quickstep next? They're bound to play one soon." Becky was dubious about that, and then decided.

"Yes. If we do just the basic until I have found my feet." I agreed, and so it was. We got out again as the band played a Quickstep, and after getting round the floor once, Becky said to try some of the more complicated steps. Again the Spin turn was easy as it's so similar to the Waltz, but it was me that messed up when we went for the Change step. That got Becky laughing, so we did it again with no mistake. I then went for the Lock step, and she sailed through.

Bands don't play for the Fox-Trot much, as so few people can do it properly. Most do a slow Quickstep instead. But tonight the band did play a Fox-Trot. It was Moonlight Serenade, one of the most beautiful tunes to dance to. Becky refused.

"I was only going to those classes long enough to have just two lessons on the Fox trot. I would mess up completely, I know." Just then a lady approached our table. She addressed Becky.

"I noticed you haven't got up to dance the Fox-Trot. Would you mind if I asked your escort to dance it with me. I noticed that he is one of the few here who can dance properly."

Becky smiled. "Of course not."

I looked at Becky. "If you don't mind?"

"No go ahead, Jack. It will be nice to see you dancing." I took the lady's hand and we went on the floor. I have to say that this lady knew how to dance. I felt like a beginner. But we got through. We stayed out for the next tune, another Fox-Trot. There were very few couples left on the floor now. I took her into the Reverse Heel turn and Weave, then a little later the Check and Weave. She followed me perfectly, and said "I was right, you do dance well."

"Oh by the way, I am Jack." I said by way of an introduction. She smiled. "Sheila." She was a little older than me, and judging by the necklace, and the rock on her finger was married to a wealthy man. It concerned me when she asked oblique questions to discover who I was, and how long I had known Becky. I must have answered the questions satisfactorily as all of a sudden she smiled and stopped asking. The reason was revealed when I escorted her back to her table. She was Richard Ewing's wife!

He looked up as if I was an intrusion, but had to recognise me as his wife took her seat next to him.

"Thank you for dancing with my wife, eh…" Sheila whispered in his ear. "Jack. You danced well."

"Thank you eh…eh...Richard." I could play him at that game.

Returning to Becky I could see that she was excited. "Do you know who that woman was?"

"Yes. It was Richard Ewing's wife. She dances well, I must say. Much better than I." Becky looked a little disappointed, as I had stolen her thunder, but she cheered up when we went back out on the floor to dance again.

"Bugger!" She exclaimed.

"Bugger what? Bugger who?" I queried. She laughed.

"Just Bugger. I really like dancing with you, Jack. And if I hadn't been so stupid back then, we could be out on this floor making people's eyes pop. And I would have done the Fox-Trot with you. That music was so romantic. Why do I bugger everything up?" She asked herself plaintively.

We stayed until the band decided that their time was up. I drove Becky home. When we got to her place she didn't get out of the car immediately. Instead she turned to me and stunned me.

"Jack, I intended to ask you if you would like to stay with me tonight. But I couldn't ask you now as your car may not be here in the morning. Can I come to your home?" Now what do you answer? Be too casual and it appears as if you don't fancy her. Be effusive and you seem as if you're desperate. I certainly wasn't going to turn her down.

"Becky, if my car was stolen I would still feel it was worth it, for having the pleasure of you." Old silver tongue, that's me. Becky laughed.

"God! Jack. You don't forget much do you?" She waited a moment. "Can I come to your home?"

I nodded. "Yes, of course."

Smiling she told me she would get some things for the morning and drive over immediately in her car. "You'll be too tired in the morning to go anywhere." Her smile was devilish.

"Promises. Promises."

CHAPTER THREE

I wasn't too tired to go anywhere the next morning, although I wouldn't have minded a few more hours in bed with Becky. When you see a beautiful woman, a beautiful naked woman walk into your bedroom, pull back the duvet and slip in beside you, it makes you think you have conquered the world. The first time with a new woman is totally exciting and totally frightening at the same time. You have to discover what she likes, what turns her on, and how she wants you to love her, both soft and gentle, which is my preference, or strong and hard. I made love to her slowly and gently.

As we lay together recovering breath, she suddenly turned in the bed and sobbed into my shoulder. I was worried. Had I done something wrong? She was muttering, mainly to herself, but I could hear some of her words.

"Oh bugger! How can I make such stupid decisions?" I heard those words and was hurt, but her next words which were to me, relieved the hurt.

"Jack. I was right when I said I should have chosen you for a Lover. When I think I could have been loved like this for the last few years, I could get quite angry with myself."

"Becky, the time wasn't right then. Perhaps the intervening years have taught us both a lesson." I could feel her nodding. Her sobs lessened as we drifted off to sleep.

Waking up in bed with a pair of beautiful breasts pressed into your side was to say the least, Heaven. I was just started to pay them the compliment of my lips and tongue when Becky leaped out of bed.

"Shit! Look at the time. I have to get to work." I have never known a woman who could shower, make up, and get dressed in so short a time.

"Do you want some breakfast?" I asked. She blew me a kiss.

"Just a coffee please" I brewed some coffee which she drank very quickly, kissed me and went to leave.

"Can I come back tonight? You started something, and I think I would like you to finish. It felt rather nice." I nodded. She smiled. "See you later."

In anticipation of Becky's arrival I had prepared a Lasagne. I expected her about seven, reasoning that she would go back to her flat first to pick up a change of clothes. She turned up at eight. I couldn't be angry as I really had little idea of how estate agents worked. Anyway, she was dressed to excite, in the black leather trousers and a sweater that did little to hide her magnificent bust. The Lasagne was a little overcooked by this time, but went down well with the Merlot I had opened. Becky helped with the clearing away and washing up. Then whilst I made coffee, she went and sat in the lounge. Her chosen place was the two seat couch, and she patted the seat beside her when I brought the coffee. I sat down and Becky immediately moved over and grabbing my head, kissed me with an open mouth. The coffee got cold, as we got hot, and very soon after we headed for bed. Becky allowed me to undress her, getting those trousers off was interesting to say the least as she wore nothing underneath them. Becky insisted that she undress me. As she got up from taking my boxers down she pushed her breasts into my face.

"You started on these this morning, and I have been thinking about it all day. Please continue."

This night was very much a repeat of last night, except that the urgency was gone. I explored and played with her body for most of the night, and Becky revelled in the attention, constantly urging me to touch her here there and everywhere. From her cries of delight I assumed she liked my caresses. The last joining was slow and easy, and the gentleness of that was very pleasing. Two lovers extracting the most out of their coupling. We both fell asleep in the early hours.

It is a lovely thing to wake in the morning and the first thing you see is a beautiful smiling face "Morning, lover." She greeted me. "If you slept as well as I did, then you had a good night." She pecked me on the mouth. "Must go and brush my teeth." She got out of bed, and I laid there in awe of her lovely body. She noticed my gaze. "Go on." She said. "Look all you want. After what you did for me last night you deserve it." She went to the bathroom. I decided that a cup of tea or coffee was exactly what I needed to restore myself to full waking mode.

"Coffee or tea?" I called to her.

"Coffee please, Jack." I went downstairs. All the lights were still on and two cups with cold coffee sat on the table in the lounge. All evidence of our rush to get into bed together. Apart from turning the lights off I did nothing except make her a coffee and for me a tea, eager to return to bed. I had thought that we would spend the day together, but not so. It was Sunday, and Becky rode on Sunday. She left telling me that she would call soon.

Was I disappointed? Well only a little. After knowing Becky for something like five years and seeing how she operated, I did not expect anything else. Becky was a user, not of drugs, but people. I had no illusions about where we were going. Nowhere! This relationship was convenient only until someone else came along who could be of more use to Becky. I thought already that I knew who that would be. Richard Ewing. For me this was being a friend, but with benefits. I got to have the naked Becky in my bed, and that was a very satisfactory benefit. It has to be said though that sex with Becky was a little one sided, she loved for me to pleasure her with my mouth; she had more orgasms that way than any other. However she would not return the compliment. Our relationship settled down into a routine. Becky was usually with me Friday nights and Saturday nights, returning to her flat during the week. That suited me, as I could get on with my hobbies, and dance on Tuesday and Thursday evenings. I had told Becky the truth, I was giving consideration to letting the dance classes lapse, but dancing with Elly was very pleasant, and there was still a little thought in my head that we may find the spark somewhere. So in some ways you could say that whilst Becky was using me, I was using her.

The proof of my theory came two months later when Becky arrived on Friday night in a very good mood. "Jack! I have got a new job."

"Hey, Becky! That's great. Who with? And what will you do?"

"I am getting into the commercial sector with Ewing and Company." In many ways I had suspected this. Hell it was obvious at the Ball what Becky was after. I just hoped that she would be happy with her success, I was happy for her, although there was this voice in my head telling me that this interlude with Becky was coming to an end. We sat down to eat, and she was so effusive, telling me all that she would be doing, about the package they had offered, the great commissions she could make, and the very real chance of promotion. That night Becky's enthusiasm about her new job spilled over into our sexual coupling, she was wild! She did a strip-tease for me immediately after our meal, and then slowly mounted the stairs, looking over her shoulder at me, her eyes seducing me with visions of Paradise. She made it to my bed a minute before I did, and she was laying there, offering herself to me. "Come on Jack. Make love to me." I did.

What is it about women that a night of unbridled sensuality energises them for the morning, whilst leaving us poor blokes wiped out? Becky was up and singing as she showered and dressed. I almost fell down the stairs, my legs felt as if they were made of rubber. She grabbed the coffee I had made then went off to work, almost skipping out of the house.

Everything was the same for the next three weeks, then one Friday afternoon Becky phoned to say she wouldn't be there that evening. "I have a viewing of some premises and could be very late to finish, so I will go home, rather than keep you waiting Jack, would it be alright to come Saturday evening?"

I told her it would be no problem. "That's fine, Becky. Hope the view goes well." I said no problem but there were two problems. First she told me that she was doing commercial sales and lettings. Now I could be wrong, but I couldn't imagine that companies looking for office space would view in the evenings. Secondly, after the first time, it was unusual for her to ask if she could come to my house. She just turned up. My antennae were vibrating. She arrived on Saturday evening and was her usual 'loving' self. I had never kidded myself that I was in any way emotional about Becky, so whatever she got up to on Friday evening was her business. I just took advantage of a willing and beautiful body.

A month went by, and the Friday evening 'viewings' were repeated twice more. I had decided that the next time it happened I was going to tell her that she wasn't welcome any more. Serendipity, chance, call it what you will, anyway it happened. On the Wednesday afternoon before the Friday I had determined to talk to Becky, my doorbell rang. I cursed as I was just in the middle of writing a rather important chapter, and it was going well. I almost decided not to respond to the doorbell, when it went again. I resigned myself to answering it. My jaw must have dropped when I saw who it was. Sheila Ewing! She smiled. "Hello Jack. Do you think we could have a chat?"

"Yes, of course. Come in." She stepped through the door and I directed her to the lounge.

"Sit down, please Sheila. Can I get you a tea or coffee?"

"A tea would be nice. Just a little milk and no sugar." Whilst I made the tea I wondered why she had come to see me, then it struck me. How did she know where I lived? Curiouser and curiouser as Alice would have said. I took the teas into the lounge, and sat down opposite her.

My thoughts in the kitchen came straight to the fore. "I am happy to see you, Sheila, but what is your purpose of calling on me? I don't recall telling you where I lived." I was a little abrupt.

"You have every right to be angry, Jack. We had what? A couple of dances together, and to presume that could be a friendship is taking the enjoyment of dancing with you too far. I found out where you lived because I had a detective follow someone who is familiar to you and to my husband. And she led him here."

"Becky!"

She nodded. And I suddenly knew what this was all about. My suspicions were confirmed. "You may know Ms. Cannon and my husband are getting together from time to time. I wouldn't call it an affair, which pre-supposes some emotional attachment. I can assure you my husband has none of that. But however much of a bastard he is, he is my husband and I want this stopped. I have evidence and photographs, but I would prefer not to use those if this can be resolved without rancour."

"You are presumably asking me if I can do anything about it."

"I hoped you could."

"Sheila. You overestimate my influence on Becky. To be honest I have had my suspicions and intended to tell her that she was no longer welcome here. I doubt that anything I could say will persuade her to stop this."

"You and Ms. Cannon are not an item then?"

"No I wouldn't describe our relationship that way. I have known her for a few years, and she and I could best be described as friends with occasional benefits." Sheila was looking down in the mouth now.

"So you can't help me?"

"I doubt I can do any good, but I will try."

"Thank you, Jack. I can't understand what she sees in him. I mean he is sixty four, and she's what, Forty or thereabouts?"

"Forty four, Sheila. But I think I know why she is seeing him. She is ambitious. She's hoping that this will pave the way for promotion and a bigger salary."

Sheila laughed a short dismissive laugh. "She'll not get that from Richard. Oh he will let her believe it, but it will never happen."

"You make it sound as if this has happened before."

"Yes. It has. I was the first, but I got pregnant, so he married me, but I can reckon on at least three others after we married."

I started smiling. Sheila looked as if she was upset that I should smile about her misfortune. "I am not smiling to hurt you, Sheila. I was smiling because the little minnow user has met the big shark user."

She saw the humour in that and smiled. "I could almost feel sorry for Becky now." She regarded me shrewdly. "And will you be there to pick up the pieces, Jack?"

I shook my head. "No. I don't know what Becky is looking for in life; I doubt that she does either. She will eventually realise that her actions are self-destructive."

"I want to teach Richard that others can play the game as well." Sheila said. "You do know that at the dance you offended him."

"No. When was that, by dancing with you?" Sheila shook her head. She was smiling when she told me.

"After you had escorted me back to my seat; which incidentally was a very gentlemanly thing to do; Richard showed you disrespect by pretending that he didn't know your name. That was intended to put you in your place. You turned it nicely, by doing the same thing. My husband thinks that he is important, and that everyone should know who he is. He was most upset about that. Now perhaps we could upset him even more."

"I'm sorry I don't know where you are going." Sheila grinned at me.

"All will be revealed, Jack. Can I come and see you next week; I would like to introduce you to my daughter, Alicia." I had no idea what was going through her mind, but had no objection to Sheila visiting again next week, if she wanted, nor meeting her daughter. "Thank you for the tea, Jack. I'm sorry I disturbed you. You are too much of a gentleman to let it show though. Alicia will like you, you know. It will make my plan so much easier." With that cryptic remark she left.

Now I had to prepare for a confrontation with Becky. I didn't want her driving over to my house, only to be told that she couldn't stay, so I decided to call her on Thursday and suggest we went for a drink. She was happy to go to a local Pub that evening, but was curious as this was out of character for me; she knew I was not one for going out drinking.

We met at six-thirty so the Pub was not busy and we could take a table with some privacy. "It's nice to go out for a drink after work, we could have done it tomorrow though, Jack."

"No, Becky we couldn't. We have been friends for quite some time, and I assure you that I do not want to end that friendship. However I don't think it possible that we can continue as we are whilst you are sleeping with Richard Ewing." Becky looked as if she had run into a wall, white-faced and aghast. I will give her credit though, she didn't lie.

"How do you know?"

"Viewing commercial properties in the evening is a bit unusual, but when they seem to occur on Friday evenings and only Friday evenings as well, that was enough for suspicion. My thoughts were confirmed when Sheila Ewing came to see me, and she has evidence."

"Oh!"

"Yes, Oh!"

"What is she going to do?"

"I suspect that she is going to let Richard know that if he goes on like this then he is going to be divorced and that will cost him dearly." Becky had to be going over in her mind how that would affect her.

"Well one way or the other it's over. We can go on as we were, Jack." In other circumstances that would have been funny. I watched her with a smile on my face whilst shaking my head.

"No Becky. That we can't. We didn't make promises of everlasting fidelity to each other, but you seemed quite happy to sleep with me, and to my mind that included an obligation. An obligation to exclusivity whilst we were together. If you had been honest with me that would have allowed me the option of accepting your actions or not. But you were not honest. I said I would like to maintain our friendship. But I don't think that I can welcome you into my home again."

I'll give her, her due. She didn't break down and cry or try to argue me away from my position. She just nodded. "Yes. I suppose that you couldn't now." She raised her eyes and looked me in the face. "I'm sorry, Jack. I thought it would advance my career. Richard was useless in bed, anyway. Not a patch on you."

"Well, Becky. I doubt that it will advance your career. In fact I suspect you will be looking for another job soon. Ewing, according to Sheila would have never given you a promotion. He just dangled the bait to get what he wanted. It's not the first time he has done that either." Now there were tears in Becky's eyes, as she realised that she had been taken for a fool.

"What the Hell am I going to do now?"

"Becky. There are lots of agencies around and about. From what I have heard and from what Sheila has said Ewing is not flavour of the month with any of them. I am sure that there is one who will want to take you on. You are good at the job, and you have a lot of background knowledge that they will find very interesting. Start ringing around. I think you may be surprised."

I could see that she was listening and rolling the idea around in her head. She nodded as if the question was resolved. "I don't deserve a friend like you, Jack. Thanks. I wish I could fall in Love with you, like you read in those Mills and Boon novels. But somehow I don't seem to have the ability to love anyone." In my head I added the words "Except yourself" but didn't say them.

Having decided her immediate future, Becky wanted to know if Sheila would take this any further.

"No. If you resign your job I think that will be enough. But she does have plans for Richard, and somehow I think she wants me involved."

"He doesn't like you, Jack. I don't know why as he hardly knows you, but he would crow when we were together about how he was having me behind your back. He would brag that he was better than you. I didn't say anything of course under the circumstances. But now I think I might find ways to let him know that he was pathetic, and that you could get me off four or five times in a night." Tears rolled down her cheeks then. "I am going to miss that. Damn!"

CHAPTER FOUR

Sheila phoned on Tuesday the following week, and we arranged for her to call on me that Thursday afternoon. I offered to go to her, but she pointed out that news of our meeting could filter through to Richard if I came to her house. She arrived promptly and introduced me to her daughter, Alicia. Now here was a surprise. In my mind I had imagined a girl in her late teens or barely in her twenties. How wrong could I be? Alicia was a confident woman and I had to guess about thirty years of age. She was also slim and very attractive, with blonde hair cut to the shoulder curling under to give a soft look. Sheila was not a tall lady and neither was her daughter. I would say they were both about five feet four. Alicia appealed to me as a younger version of my dance partner, Elli. She smiled as she held her hand out to shake.

"Hello, Jack. I am very pleased to meet you. I have heard about your dancing skills from Mum, and I hope to be able to experience that for myself." I was nonplussed; could it be that Alicia was in on Sheila's plan? A plan that I had no knowledge of! Sheila could see that I was in the dark.

"Jack, let's sit down and I'll explain. Alicia will make us a drink. That is if you don't mind her messing in your kitchen?"

"Eh, No! Not at all. If you prefer something stronger, there's a bottle of Chardonnay in the fridge. I could open that." Alicia seemed happy about that.

"Great. A glass of that would go down well. Don't worry, Jack. I'll find everything."

Sheila and I sat down, making some small talk until Alicia came back, with three glasses, and the bottle. She poured the wine and it was time for Sheila to reveal her plan. I looked at her expectantly. "Jack I know that Ms. Cannon resigned on Friday. I am sure that was your doing, so thank you very much. My husband is aware that I know what he was up to, and is treading on egg-shells at the moment. He is behaving himself for now, but I am certain that given time his arrogance will allow him to think that he can get away with it once more. My plan is to dent his arrogance severely, and then I will have him understand exactly what will happen if he does this again."

I could see what she wanted to achieve. "I understand that Sheila. But you seem to be involving me in your plan. I can't imagine how I could be of assistance."

"What do you think is Richard's most precious possession?"

I shrugged my shoulders. "I have no idea."

"I'll tell you. It's Alicia."

I wasn't too surprised to hear that. "I would expect that most fathers would count their daughter as precious."

Alicia replied instead of Sheila. "They do, Jack. But my father is obsessive about it. I am thirty-five." Now that was a surprise. "I have a job, a good job, not in father's business either, my own flat, and I am independent. But he will not let me go. He phones me every evening about nine, to see what sort of day I have had. If I'm out, he will continue to phone every hour to see if I'm back, and ask questions to discover if anyone is with me. He will also turn up at my flat unannounced. He has embarrassed me and any boyfriends I may have had. With that sort of attention they don't last long. Do you get the picture?"

I did get the picture, and Sheila nodded as she saw understanding come to me. "So Jack. What do you think he would feel if he saw Alicia out and enjoying the company of a man he dislikes?"

"Pretty angry, I should think."

"Yes he would. Particularly if it was the man who got for free and willingly, that for which he had to offer a fictitious bribe. That would humiliate him. He targeted Becky after that Ball, you know. You had slighted him, and he had to get back at you, taking the woman he believed to be yours would do the trick."

Now was the time to give this some thought, before I got into something that may take me out of my depth. Ewing would dislike me even more, that didn't trouble me in the slightest, but what measures could he take to get even? I didn't think there were any. Sheila it would seem could read my mind.

"He can't do anything about it, Jack. His usual tactic is to interfere in your business, undercut you and things like that. But you can't suffer, I believe that you have independent means. Anyway I would let him know that any revenge would rebound on him, big time."

Then Alicia added some words of comfort. "I will make sure that my father understands that any action he takes will be against me, not just at you." They waited for my response. I realised that my being seen with Alicia; which was not distasteful to me, actually quite the opposite; had to be a public event or at anyway an event when all Ewing's friends and competitors could see his humiliation.

"Where and when do you see this taking place?"

Sheila smiled, I hadn't said yes, but even asking that question was an indication that I may well say yes. "There is a charity Ball for Cancer research, in about four weeks. I shall get you tickets for two. He won't know that Alicia will be there with you. When he does see you and her together, he will bust a gut!" Alicia then added her contribution.

"I will be all over you, Jack. Will that be hard to take?"

I laughed. "Oh I think I could manage that, as long as you have the paramedics on stand-by." She smiled, accepting the inferred compliment. "But I hope you are a good actress." I finished.

Alicia was shaking her head. "Oh no. Jack. I have a hunch that I won't be acting. Mum says you are a good dancer, and I'm looking forward to dancing with you." I may have looked sceptical, after all women of her age don't tend to do Ballroom. By way of explanation she added. "Mum has been teaching me for years. It will be great to dance with a man, instead of bosom to bosom."

I gave them my decision. "Very well. I think the plan is fraught with difficulties, but I will go along with it."

Sheila was relieved, and Alicia seemed happy as well. Sheila held her empty glass up. "This Chardonnay was very nice, any chance of another?" Alicia did the honours once again, and we toasted to the success of the scheme. Alicia asked if she could have a look round, and with my permission she wandered off, while I continued chatting with Sheila. Suddenly Alicia was back.

"Mum! You must come and look at this." Sheila got up and followed Alicia into the conservatory. I walked over to the lounge window to see what had excited Alicia. They were looking at the Treadmill. I had started going to a gym when I retired, but got fed up with the continued hike in rates, coupled with the fact that very often you had to wait between routines to get on the next machine. I already had a rowing machine, so I invested in a good treadmill.

Sheila came back into the lounge. "No wonder you don't look your age, Jack. Do you get on there often?"

"Every day."

"I'm impressed. We all talk about keeping fit, but few go the extent of actually doing something about it." I looked out to the conservatory again, as I heard the treadmill start. Alicia had kicked off her shoes and was walking at a slow pace. I grinned to Sheila.

"Come on, we'll give her a surprise.

We went and stood beside the machine.

"Enjoying it?" I asked Alicia.

She smiled and said. "It's great." She looked at her mum. "I ought to get one of these, but I couldn't in the flat. All the neighbours would complain at the noise." Whilst she was talking to Sheila, I reached over and touched the button for a much faster speed. The machine went quickly from three kilometres per hour to seven. Unable to adjust to the faster speed, Alicia started travelling backwards. I got to the back of the machine just in time, and caught Alicia as she stumbled off with a yelp of surprise. She recovered, but didn't seem too anxious to stand on her own feet for a while.

"I'm sorry." I said. "That wasn't very clever of me to do that."

Alicia didn't seem upset by the trick. "Oh I don't know. It's not so bad if you fall into a man's arms. I could do that often if you like." She winked at me. I couldn't believe it. Alicia was flirting with me.

Sheila joined in the fun. "Alicia! I didn't bring you up to throw yourself at a man like that. Shame on you."

Just before they left, Alicia needed the bathroom. Whilst we waited Sheila remarked. "Alicia likes you, Jack. It's all going to work beautifully."

I wasn't quite sure in what context her mind was working. But one question was bugging me.

"Sheila, I know you dance well, but how well does Alicia dance?"

"I don't think you have to worry about that. I have been teaching Alicia ballroom since she was fifteen. She's good, she knows all the steps. Possibly not as proficient as you, but she won't let you down.

You lead well. It may be a good idea if you got together before the Ball. Get her used to the hold and framing when dancing with a man. I want you and her to look as if you were born to dance together."

I nodded in agreement. "Perhaps she would like to come to the dance classes I attend, two or three times. That could help."

Sheila shook her head in rejection of that idea. "Could she come here? You have plenty of room, and I think she would be more comfortable that way."

"No problem. If she gives me a call when it's suitable, we'll arrange it."

Fate protect me from a woman who was after revenge. I should not have been surprised with Sheila's attitude, from what she had told me Ewing treated her with disdain. I have heard so many horror stories from men and husbands who have been victim of a woman's retribution. It did occur to me that I was only part of Sheila's plan. What else there was I would probably not know until the trap was sprung. But in the meantime I had the distinct pleasure of dancing with Alicia. Now that was something to look forward to.

Alicia called two days later to ask if she could come and practice that evening. I had no plans so we agreed that she would be at my house around seven.

"Will you want to eat?" I asked her.

"Thanks, Jack but no. I will have had something for lunch so I will be fine."

"OK."

"Jack?"

"Yes?"

"If I brought my sweats, would it be alright with you if I spent a bit of time on your rowing machine and treadmill?"

"Help yourself. I get my exercise in the morning, so you won't inconvenience me in any way."

"That's great. See you later, Jack."

Alicia arrived at ten to seven. She wore a rather attractive frilly blouse with long sleeves, and a full skirt, suitable for dancing. When I greeted her as Alicia, she informed me in no uncertain terms that I should call her Ally. "My father insists that everyone calls me Alicia. I prefer for my friends to call me Ally." She paused for a moment. "Well those friends that my father has not frightened away."

"OK, Ally. Your wish is my command." I had bought some CD's when I first started dancing. They were by Victor Sylvester's orchestra. He had been a champion dancer between the wars, and was insistent on strict tempo, so the music was good for dance. I put one on and we listened for a few minutes, then I turned it off. Ally looked surprised.

"Before we dance, we must get the hold right." I took up the position. "Now see how my shoulders and arms are. My left arm is forty-five degrees to the floor, and the palm up. You lay your right hand in my palm. Don't grasp it, just lay it on." She did. "Now your left hand should rest on top of my right upper arm, again don't grasp it, just rest it there."

"Like this?" Ally asked.

"Yes. That's good. Now my right arm will go round your back and rest just below your shoulder blades." I demonstrated. We were not face to face, but slightly off-set, an interesting position as Ally was pressing her right breast into my chest, possibly a little more pressure than was needed, and she was smiling mischievously.

"Now arch your back slightly, your bosom and my chest should not actually touch, but that position brings our hips together. That is how I lead you, with my hips, and gentle pressure on your back. If I sway into the direction we need to go, you will feel that immediately." Ally was grinning.

"What will I feel immediately, Jack?" She rubbed her hips suggestively side to side.

"Ally. The idea is to piss your dad off, not get him excited." Ally chuckled.

"Is it alright then, if you get excited?"

"I doubt that I will."

"Oh!" Her voice expressed disappointment.

"Not because my partner isn't attractive at all. But because I will be very aware of your father's eyes shooting daggers at me."

"Well then, I see I have a challenge." She was smiling innocently. How do women manage to seem so innocent and yet still insinuate really sexy suggestions at the same time?

I had to get this back on track. "Now your head. Tilt back slightly and turn it to the side." Ally followed the instructions and took the hold well. "Now let's dance. Shall we start with the Waltz?"

"Yes. That's an idea, keep it simple at first." I put the music on. Ally did know all the steps, and we practiced the combinations that would allow us to float round the ballroom seemingly at ease. After an hour we decided to take a break.

"Tea, Coffee, Wine or water? What's your choice, Ally?"

"Tea please, Jack." She came into the kitchen as I prepared the drink.

"That was good." She said. "I was surprised that the hold seemed to make the whole thing smoother. And I definitely felt your lead." She smirked. "Not the lead I would have liked though."

"Ally! Let's get this straight. We are dancing for a purpose. It's your mother's idea, and I am certain that it is not part of her plans that we do anything else but dance and upset your father. OK?" I was astonished when she smiled.

"Mum said you were a gentleman, and she's right. Now I can tell her that you would not consider trying anything with me." She stepped towards me and put her hand on my arm. "But a little bit of flirting would be OK, wouldn't it, Jack?"

"I suppose. But not too much. I don't want your boyfriends coming after me." She shook her head.

"None of those. I get fed up with fending off men who seem to think I am their way in to favour with my father. And as I said they don't last very long."

We sat down to drink the tea. "Jack. Did you love that woman you were seeing, Becky, wasn't it?"

"No, Ally. I have known Becky for years. It was odd really. We had always got on well, and it was quite a surprise when it got physical. I didn't think it would last, and I am sure now that Becky didn't think that either."

"Mum thinks she was a fool. I mean to give you up to screw my father. Trading down I call that."

"Thank you, Ally. But as I said it was never going anywhere, so perhaps she thought she saw a chance for something better."

"What! To become my father's mistress?"

"Well as my mistress, she wasn't going to benefit in any way. I've got nothing."

"I don't know what you class as nothing. But I reckon you have qualities that are priceless."

"You're kind, Ally. But mistaken. You don't know me well enough to make that judgement."

She just grinned at me. "I will have to get to know you better, and I am sure that my opinion will be justified." I had finished my tea and suggested we get back to dance.

We danced for another half an hour. When we decided that was sufficient for the first evening. "Can I work out on your treadmill now, Jack?"

"Yes, of course."

Ally got the bag she had brought. "I've got some sweats and trainers in here, if it's OK with you; I'll pop up to the bathroom and change."

"Go ahead." Ten minutes later Ally came down. She had said sweats, but what she was wearing bore little relationship to the accepted version of 'sweats'. A thin tee shirt and very short shorts. She gave me a smile as she went through to the sun-room, as I had a mini heart-attack. Oh, those long svelte legs! Then I heard the treadmill start. I went up to my office and played around with my writing, not successfully, as my mind was too busy with pictures of Ally. I knew I could not get anything worthwhile written, but it was better than hanging around trying to get glimpses of her working out. I did manage to get some cohesive sentences down when a voice addressed me from the door.

"Mum said something about you writing. What do you write?"

"Short stories mainly, but I have been working on a novel for something like five years." I looked up at her. Oh God! Her Tee was soaked through with sweat, and she wasn't wearing a bra. I suggested that she took a shower.

"Whilst you're in there I will make us a drink."

"OK. But don't make tea for me, I'll just have water. I need to re-hydrate."

She came down and took a long drink from the glass of water. She sat opposite me in the lounge. "Did I embarrass you?"

"No."

"Well, why didn't you look at me? Most men would have when I was soaked with perspiration like that."

"Ally, you are a damned fine looking woman, no, a beautiful young woman, and I am just a normal man, a middle aged man. Of course I want to look at you, but I couldn't do that without wishing, and life has taught me that wishes are fishes. They usually swim away." Ally was pensive for a few moments.

"Sometime wishes do come true, Jack."

"Mine don't." I said sourly. Ally changed the topic. I was thankful else it could have got into difficult territory.

"You said you worked out in the mornings. What time would that be?"

"Usually about half past seven, why?"

"It would probably be better for me to work out early. I suspect the adrenalin will keep me awake most of the night. Can I come at that time?"

What the hell was going on here, I asked myself. I was trying to do her mother a favour, and that could cause me a problem. Now here was Ally assuming that she had the right to use my equipment whenever she wanted. Unfortunately I couldn't think of any reason to say no. I have been told in the past that I allowed myself to be inconvenienced in order to do others a favour. I seemed to be going down that road yet again. However the road looked very attractive from where I sat. "Well it's up to you. You are the one getting up early." She smiled.

"That's settled then. Thanks, Jack."

I was half-expecting Ally to arrive the next morning, but she didn't. I had that funny emotion of relief and disappointment vying for possession of my mind. She phoned me early that evening. "Hi, Jack. Did you have a good day?"

"Yeah. Not too bad. How about you?"

"Busy really, but boring. I need to cheer up so can I come over tomorrow evening for some more dance practice?"

"Yes, of course. What dance?"

"The Fox-Trot please, Jack. Mum says you do that well."

"OK, Ally. The Fox-Trot it will be."

She arrived at seven, and we got on with the practice. Again, Ally knew the steps; it was the timing that needed practice, and the Heel

Turn, a most difficult manoeuvre. She had proper leather soled and heeled dance shoes but even so we practiced in the conservatory as it had a laminated wooden floor. Better that than the heel turns ripping up my carpet. We worked on that and the Hover, a hesitation step. Our practice went on for almost two hours, and I decided to call it over then.

"Phew! That takes it out of you." she remarked. I was grinning.

"Yes, but don't forget, you will never be doing that for two hours in the ballroom. More like six minutes maximum."

"Thank God for that!" I was making us some tea. Ally joined me in the kitchen. She was looking around, and opened the fridge to get some milk. She couldn't help noticing the foodstuffs I had. "Do you cook all this yourself?"

"Yes."

That started her thinking. "You really don't need a woman in your life, do you, Jack?" Strange comment I thought.

"Well it depends, why a man needs a woman. Cooking, cleaning, and shopping. None of these are rocket science. If a man needs a woman purely for those reasons then he's lost sight of what is important about relationships." Ally had a little smile on her face, I realised that she had succeeded in drawing me out.

"So what other reasons are there, Jack? Apart from Sex."

"We all have reasons, Ally. They vary from person to person. It's no sugar for you isn't it?"

"No thanks." She grinned. "You're now supposed to say I am sweet enough already."

"Oh I expect you have heard that so often it's become boring."

"Yes. But coming from you it would be sincere."

I made no reply and picked up the mugs and took them through to the lounge. "Sorry, Jack. I embarrassed you."

"Forget it Ally. Where you were going seemed inappropriate, that's all." Ally was deep in thought for a while as we sipped tea. Finally she lifted her head as if her mind was made up.

"Not inappropriate, Jack. Possibly presumptive."

"Oh?"

"Yes." Ally continued. "I like you, Jack. I know this thing is supposed to be about getting back at my father, and it will. But for me it has bonus. I will be dancing with a really nice guy. A guy I am starting to like a lot, and who I would hope could get to like me as well. That's where the presumption came in."

"I see." I couldn't think of anything else to say at that moment, and a non-committal reply seemed the best thing to say, whilst I tried to sort this out in my head. Where was she going?

CHAPTER FIVE

Over the next three weeks Ally called frequently in the evening to practice our dancing. She also got into the habit of arriving around seven-thirty every other morning to get on the treadmill and rowing machine. I changed my workout times to seven, so that I could shower when she was working out. Ally noticed this change without comment. For me it was all about avoiding temptation. Most men would relish the opportunity to see a woman like Ally, soaking in sweat, rendering her tee-shirt almost transparent, and I am no different. However I realised that although Ally seemed quite happy to show me, the chances of going further were minimal and I would not be able to get on with my writing or anything else if remembrances of Ally's exquisite breasts were to continually occupy my mind.

There were just a few days remaining before this charity ball, and our practice had become superfluous. I had no doubt that she would look fantastic on the ballroom floor. So it was that we practiced only for a short time that last week and fell into conversation more. It was good as we found a lot to talk about. We argued about politics, we agreed on the need to preserve the countryside, and we discussed attitudes and the bigotry that still existed in the world. I asked questions and challenged some of her attitudes; she didn't take umbrage, rather the opposite, pleased to defend herself. However it was one ordinary question that I asked which opened Pandora's Box. "You told me that you had your own work, and that it wasn't related to your father's business, but didn't tell me what you do."

Ally was silent for a while, deep in thought, and then answered. "I'm a Model." From the way she looked and dressed that wasn't surprising, but I couldn't understand why she had taken so long to answer.

"I'm not surprised, Ally. From my point of view you are perfect for that sort of work." She was shaking her head.

"No, Jack. You don't understand. I am not a clothes horse model. I am a photographic model, a glamour model."

My understanding of that was models who posed in bikini's or occasionally topless. So naively said. "You would make any bikini look good."

She smiled. "Thank you, it's nice of you to say that. But I rarely wear any clothes when I am working."

The expression dumbstruck was the perfect description for me at that moment. I sat there and I am certain that my mouth hung open, unable to say a word. Ally said the word. "I guess Gob-smacked is appropriate, isn't it, Jack?" After I had gathered my composure I nodded.

"I think it is the right word, surprise, bombshell, and astonishment, all of those things as well."

"But not disgust, you didn't say disgust."

"No, Ally. Why should I say disgust? I haven't got to my age without realising that someone's got to pose for the photographs in magazines that I have read. If I didn't feel disgust for my actions in buying and reading them, then it would be hypocritical for me to label the girls who posed. Neither do I suppose that the women who pose are automatically of loose morals."

The expression on Ally's face was happiness. She came over to where I sat and kissed me. "Thank you, Jack. I was so worried about telling you. I nearly didn't you know. But my head was telling me that you would understand and not think badly of me. My head was right. When we are in bed together I will tell you all about it."

"Whoa! Stop right there. Who said anything about our going to bed together? We dance together, and that is simply to put an earthquake under your father. That's it." Ally didn't agree, I could tell from her expression. Oh hell, another determined woman!

"Listen to me, Jack. Let me tell you a little about myself. The men I have been out with tend to fall into two categories. The Lickspittles who dance to my father's tune, or who want to earn brownie points with him. And the Golden boys, as I call them. Men who believe themselves handsome, who cannot pass a mirror without an admiring glance at themselves. Men who believe that it is their right to have a good looking girl on their arm. I've been there; Jack and I felt demeaned, angry with myself for boosting their self-image or their ambitions. The men I would really like to know don't ask me out." Ally stopped to drink some tea; I said nothing as I was sure she would go on. But I was aware of part of the problem. How often did I not approach a pretty girl when I was young as I thought she would not be interested in plain Jack Hunter?

"Jack. I like you because you are none of those things. I like you because you talk to me as a person, an equal whose opinions are just as important as your own, just think back over our conversation this evening." She grinned. "And you talk to my face, not at my tits! I like you Jack because when I flirt you blush. When I pushed my breast into you when we were in hold, you pulled away even though I am sure you didn't find it unpleasant. You value me as a person, not as a body."

Was it my turn to say something? Frankly I didn't know what to say, so what I said was disjointed as I was thinking as I talked. "Ally. You have just thrown me totally. I did not think for one moment that you could feel any connection with someone of my……"

She interrupted. "If you say age, I shall scream!" Her eyes were blazing. "What has age got to do with how someone feels?" She looked upwards as if appealing for help from above. "Jack, all I want is to know you better, become a close friend, and if we do go to bed together, I'm not saying we will, but if we do is that the end of the world? Or don't you want to see me naked in your bed? My father has tried his best to control my life, and has browbeaten and manipulated the men I go out with. He cannot do that with you, you proved that when you dissed him that time. And it's your maturity that allows you to do all of that."

"If you had let me finish, I was going to say my situation." I tried to keep the smile off my face. Of course I was going to say age, but I thought I would muddy the waters a little.

Ally seemed at first to be surprised, and then she smiled. "Oh yes you were."

"Oh no I wasn't" She was laughing now, and I had no option but to join in her laughter.

"Bastard!" She cried. For the next few minutes it was impossible to get a sensible word out of either of us. The moment one of us tried the look on the other's face would set off the laughter again. Eventually I got control of myself enough to get words out.

"I'll go and get my calendar and red pen." Ally looked mystified, so I explained.

"Well it will be a red letter day."

"What will?"

"The day you get into my bed, naked. I must make sure I am here to see it." I managed to keep my face straight. Ally didn't. She was laughing again.

Ally left about ten-thirty giving me a full open mouthed kiss as she left. "Just a taster, Jack." She teased. She left me with a problem, was I going to sleep that night? Probably not. My dilemma would be not so much did I want to go to bed with Ally? Of course I did, what man wouldn't? Well those blokes who walked the other side of the street may not, but most other men would give their souls for the chance. I had to think forward. If I did get into a relationship with Ally, I would not want it to end. I mean, take a man to paradise and he will want to stay there wouldn't he? Ally was probably of a different view that we could have fun together and when someone better, someone nearer her age came along, move on. Yet the delights that I would find with her were a pressing temptation. Needless to say I didn't sleep well that night and got out of bed at six-thirty feeling like shit! I had two showers that morning, one to wake me up, and another after I had worked out and I still didn't know what to do. Eventually I had a plan. It wasn't much of a plan but would have to do. Get this bloody Ball out of the way, then sit down with Ally and talk it through.

I collected Ally from her apartment, at eight the evening of the Ball. With Sheila's input we had decided that it would suit their plans if we made an entrance after most people were there, so that if Richard was going to make a scene then he would have to do it with a large audience. Ally left her coat at the cloak room then came to join me in the Lobby. You could feel the stir as she came through the crowd. Angels have that effect, don't they? She was wearing a pale gold dress, which contrasted well with her tanned skin. It was full skirted fitting her small waist closely. The bodice, well almost a bodice, consisted of a narrow choker collar from which two broad straps came down only meeting when they reached her waist, There was nothing under them except Ally, pure Ally. She smiled and twirled. Oh shit! There was no back to the dress and the straps over her shoulders didn't cover her sides, the swell of her breasts below her arms were very evident.

"Like it?" She asked.

"It's almost as beautiful as you. But I've no bloody idea where I am going to put my hand when we are dancing."

"I could give you some suggestions, Jack. But I doubt that it would be proper when we're dancing though." Her eyes were twinkling.

I grinned. "I suspect that your suggestions could be interesting but, as you say not entirely proper." There was a smirk on her face. "So come on, let's go into the Lion's Den. Hail Caesar, we who are about to die, salute you!"

Sheila had thoughtfully reserved a table for us, and we made it without fuss. A waitress appeared and took an order for drinks. We had just taken the first sip, when a little murmur made me look up. Ewing was making a beeline for our table. I told Ally as she had her back to him. She grinned.

"The fun's starting." Ewing arrived at our table and ignored me, even though I stood. He addressed Ally.

"Alicia! I didn't realise that you would be here this evening. You should have let me know. But never mind, I have room at my table, so come and join us." Ally looked up.

"Hello Daddy. I believe you know Jack Hunter. If Jack is happy, we could join you for a short while." Ewing looked at me as if I was something foul that he had stepped in.

"I doubt that we will have room for him. He won't mind though, if you join us." Ally smiled sweetly at him.

"Oh no. Daddy, I couldn't desert my escort for the evening. That would be discourteous."

Ewing was getting angry now, and as his anger built, so did the onlookers who anticipated some sort of confrontation. "Alicia, I will not brook any argument. Do as you are told."

"No." Ally said this vehemently. I thought it time for me to get involved. As calmly as I could I told him.

"Ewing! You are making a scene. Ally is old enough to know her own mind, and she accepted my invitation to be here this evening. Do allow her the right to make her own decisions." He rounded on me. His anger obvious in his eyes.

"Be quiet you upstart. This has nothing to do with you." He spoke to Ally again.

"Alicia. This person is totally unsuited to be with you. Look at him he must be much older than you. Now see sense and come and join my table." He had not noticed Sheila joining the group around our table. Until she spoke from just behind him.

"Richard! How much older than Ms. Cannon were you, when you got her into bed?" She said it loud enough for the comment to be heard by the immediate onlookers.

Ewing's face showed shock. Sheila went on. Quieter now, but with steel in her voice.

"You are sixty four. I believe the lady was forty four, but Mr. Hunter could confirm that, couldn't you, Jack?"

I nodded. "Yes. She was."

Sheila went on remorselessly. "So if you didn't consider Ms. Cannon too young for you, you can hardly claim that Mr. Hunter is too old for Alicia?" Ewing's anger was such that logical thought had flown.

"Has he been putting around slander?" He pointed at me, his finger wavering as his blood pressure rose.

"No. Ewing I haven't. Why should I bother? You aren't really worth talking about." I understood that would hit his inflated ego. Beside me I heard Ally clamp down on a short laugh.

Before Ewing could explode at me Sheila got his attention. "Richard!" She spoke sharply. "Mr. Hunter has said nothing about you to anyone. I on the other hand can, as I have the evidence of your little trysts. Now if you don't want them made public I suggest you come back to our table and calm down." Ewing could not resist making one more comment.

"Lay one hand on my daughter, and I will have you in Court to answer charges."

I laughed. But Ally had something to say. "Daddy. If Jack lays a hand on me, it will be with my complete agreement and encouragement. In fact I rather look forward to it. And I will be quite happy to stand up in your court and tell them so." Ewing left his face puce with anger. Sheila gave us a smile.

"Well done, and thank you Jack." Then she followed in his wake. The small crowd that had gathered broke up, but not without some gleeful grins for the way that Ewing had been taken down a peg.

I sat down to see the beaming smile on Ally's face. She leaned across and kissed me. "Jack, you were great. Not saying too much, but what you said was perfect, and you kept your dignity. My father lost his, but you remained the gentleman."

I had many questions, but one was paramount. "Ally. When we talk you always call him father, and then when he was standing there you called him daddy?"

Ally looked a little sad then gave me the answer. "I call him father, because he is my biological father. I only called him daddy to remind him that I was his little girl but I was seeing another man to whom I may give my body. That will hurt him. It may not make sense in your mind, but it does in mine, and I expect in Mum's mind as well." I thought about that, and she was right. It didn't make sense to me.

The band had not been playing for a while, now they started up with a quickstep. I got up and turned to Ally.

"May I have the pleasure of this dance?" I held my hand out. Ally placed her hand in mine.

"I would be delighted." The floor soon got crowded, the quickstep was a popular dance and the tempo could be used for many modes of dance. We got round the floor quickly, apart from a couple of occasions when I had to throw in a spin turn to avoid first a couple who suddenly stopped dancing, then another who were jiving. Ally was smiling broadly.

"I love this, it's brilliant." I would have loved it as well, but I could feel the hatred of Ewing's eyes as we circled in the corner nearest to his table. Ally flashed him a beautiful smile as we spun, letting him know that she was enjoying herself.

We did all of the ballroom dances, quickstep, fox-trot, tango and waltz. It wasn't the last waltz, but nearing the end when many couples had left, so there was an almost empty floor for us. I let loose with that waltz, and Ally followed me perfectly. All the different steps that we couldn't do on a crowded floor, we did then. I was having a ball at the Ball. I didn't notice at first, nor did Ally, but the other dancers had stopped and were standing there watching us, the band leader noticed and reprised the melody more than once. I saw that Ally had realised what was happening and a look of fear crossed her face. I whispered to her.

"You are dancing better than any of them, just enjoy." After the next spin, I moved into a sway across my body, Ally followed so elegantly, raising the free leg and pointing her toe gracefully at the nadir of the sway. We came back into hold and then I lead her into a series of natural turns. A little like a Viennese Waltz. Her full skirt flowed outwards as we turned and turned adding drama to the dance. At last the leader decided that the set had to end, and with the last chords I let Ally out of hold and spun her. She seemed to realise my intentions and twirling on her toes, sank down, her skirts surrounding her in a perfect circle. I still held her one hand, and as the music faded away bowed slightly from the shoulders, bent and kissed the back of her hand. Ally looked up; her eyes glistened with happiness, as the onlookers burst into applause. I nodded my thanks for the applause and lifted Ally to her feet, tucked her arm undermine, and led her back to our table.

Within two minutes Sheila was there, bubbling with excitement. Taking Ally's hand, she clasped it to her breast.

"All those years, Ally, all those years and I never thought for one moment I would ever be able to see you dance so beautifully. That was magic!" She turned to me.

"Jack. Thank you."

I shook my head. "Sheila. I was told once that the only reason a man led the ballroom dance was to show his partner's grace and elegance. The man makes the frame, his partner is the picture. Ally was grace, elegance and beauty personified tonight, a perfect picture. So you don't have to thank me. "

Sheila smiled. "Gentleman Jack."

"Mum." Ally had a question. "Is my father going to be difficult?"

"Oh no. I told him some of what I know, and also what my solicitor could do to him in court. He will behave himself. But I have to tell you he was enthralled when he saw you dancing. It was spoilt for him because you were dancing with Jack. He will just have to live with it." She leant over and kissed Ally, then gave me a kiss on the cheek.

"You make a lovely couple." Then she was off.

The band announced the last waltz and Ally looked at me expectantly. "Are you going to ask me for the last dance, Jack?"

I shook my head. "No."

"Oh! Why?"

"Because you just asked me, and I accept." We went out onto the floor, and I offered the hold.

Ally shook her head. "Not formal this time, Jack. Hold me close please?" I had little choice really, as she crept into my arms and wrapped her arms around my neck. There was only one place for me to put my arms, and that was around her waist, my fingers on her bare skin.

"This is nice." She sighed. We moved slowly, any idea of proper steps, gone out of the window. Like everyone else we shuffled, swayed and moved around in a small circle. Ally tightened her arms and made sure that her breasts were tucked right into my chest. I could feel her nipples like darts, and she emphasised the contact by moving slightly from side to side. The understandable reaction for any man was an excitement, and mine became known to her. She moved her belly, testing it.

"Now that does feel very nice. Did I do that?" She asked cheekily.

"Who else is rubbing themselves against me?" I asked rhetorically.

"Oh, good. Now I know you do react to me."

"Yes, and if you don't behave yourself the next reaction will be a spanked bottom."

"Is that before or after I get into your bed naked?" I could feel her shaking with repressed laughter. I had a chuckle as well.

"No. My discipline says smack the bottom first then send the culprit to bed alone, without supper."

"That's no fun." She looked up at me and pulled a face.

The band played their final chord and that was that. We went through the crush to get Ally's coat, and I held it as she slipped her arms through. My car was in the car park, about three hundred yards away, she insinuated her arm through mine and hugged it as we walked. It took about twenty minutes to drive to her flat and that was done in silence. I walked her to the door.

"Coffee?" She asked, and I hesitated. She smiled at me.

"It's just coffee and a chat. Not coffee and......' Her voice tailed away.

"Coffee and a chat will be good."

CHAPTER SIX

Ally's flat was very impressive. It was open plan, in a minimalist style, with laminated wooden floors, leather couch, individual chairs, and glass-top occasional tables. There was a balcony from which the lights of the town could be seen about two miles away. I followed her into a kitchen of gleaming chrome and black granite work surfaces; everything was pristine as if food preparation could not sully its magnificence. Not for Ally was there a kettle and granule coffee, she got out a large cafetiere and poured hot water onto ground coffee. She smiled as she carried the cafetiere, cream, sugar and cups on a tray through to the lounge. Women do like to make a ritual out of these things. She poured the coffee.

"Like it?"

I assumed she was referring to the flat. "Yes, very impressive. Modelling must pay well."

"No. modelling didn't pay for this. My grandmother did though." she looked at me with a question on her face. "Jack I am going to change, I don't want to sit around in this dress. I assure you I am not going to change into the proverbial 'something more comfortable' just something more comfortable." She giggled. "If you know what I mean." I laughed too.

"When I was young at this point I would be checking that I had a condom in my wallet, then I would take off my jacket and loosen my tie to be ready." She grinned.

"Take off your jacket, and loosen your tie by all means, but you won't need the condom." She went off to change. At the last minute she turned smiling. "Only one condom?" She shook her head and went in to the bedroom. I took off my jacket, and loosened my tie. It was a proper bow tie that I had tied myself, so pulling one end undid the bow and the two tails hung down from under my collar. Taking my cup I walked over to the picture window. During the day this view would be superb, but at night it was tremendous.

"Good view, isn't it?" Ally had come up behind me. I nodded.

"That would put a premium on the price. You must have a generous grandmother." I turned, and she had slipped into something comfortable, but hardly alluring. A brushed cotton top with long sleeves and matching slacks.

"Sexy." I said.

She grinned. "Told you." She sipped her coffee. "She was mum's mum. She died before I was born, although she knew mum was pregnant. I was so surprised when I was twenty-one, and the solicitor wrote to tell me that she had made me a bequest. Mum didn't know about it either."

"That's sad. She would love to have known you, and you her."

Ally looked at me in surprise. "Isn't that typical of you. Most men I know would have talked about the bequest. You are sad that I never knew her. You have a lovely heart!" She turned away and sat down on the couch, tucking her legs underneath her. For a moment I saw her eyes glass with moisture.

"Mum inherited a lot from her. That's what got my father started on his expansion. Before that he only had one office." That explained why Sheila was so confident she could pull Ewing back into line.

"Did you ever think about going into the business?" I asked.

"God! No." She was quiet for a moment. "I know we are supposed to love our parents, and I think in some way that I do love my father, but I don't like him at all. That dislike prevents me from ever getting close to him so I have no idea if I really love him or not. Do you find that strange, Jack?"

"No. I know of quite few people who feel the same. I suppose I loved my parents. My dad was quite successful but I rarely saw him. He was always off on some business trip somewhere. He wouldn't buy me anything until he thought I had earned it. It was a lesson that I learned. When I grew up, I didn't look to him for help at all, as I didn't think I would get it. I made my own way. OK I wasn't as successful as he was. But I had enough for all my needs and some of my wants."

"That's an interesting way of words. Enough for all my needs, and some of my wants." She pondered. "That's a good philosophy for a contented life. I like it." She examined me as if she had never seen me before. "That must be why you are such a lovely man, Jack. I could never pin it down before. Now I know why I like you so much." She waited for me to say something. I didn't. It had always been a tactic when I worked to allow others to talk, you listened and learned things, and that gave you the edge you needed to make a sale. Having decided that I wasn't commenting, Ally went on.

"I am not a virgin, Jack. But I am not that experienced. I told you about the men I seemed to attract. Few got into my panties. I have always felt an attraction to older men, men who were assured of themselves, comfortable with who they were. Men who would be more interested in me, rather than as a dressing on their arm. There's not many of those around unfortunately. Then you came along. As I got to know you I began ticking the boxes, and the more I knew you the more boxes got ticked. I liked you from the start, then liking turned into something else, an emotion I had never felt before. Jack! I am a very short journey away from falling in Love with you, and I am close to doing what Mum said I shouldn't do, throwing myself at a man. Please Jack; if I did that would you catch me?"

I crossed the room and sat beside Ally, taking her hand in mine. "Ally, you are a beautiful woman, but more importantly you are beautiful inside. Any man would be happy to know you and love you. But, you know so little about me. I was divorced because I cheated on my wife. I have a daughter I haven't seen in years. I have had long term relationships that come to nothing. So you can see I am not a good bet. Somehow relationships don't work for me. Don't think about throwing yourself at me unless you have a safety net." Ally's eyes narrowed.

"I knew you would do that. Put yourself down. Right! You cheated because your wife was an incurable alcoholic. Your cheating was not a quick affair, you wanted a permanent relationship, and she didn't. You had other relationships after you were divorced, but they were long-term. All of this tells me that you were not playing the field, you wanted permanence. That's what I want as well."

I was very surprised. How did Ally know all this? I asked her. "You seem to know a lot about me. I have never mentioned any of this, so how did you come by the information?" She smiled. You know that smile a woman has when she has a secret? The smile that says women are superior, even though they allow us to believe the opposite.

"I talked to Becky."

"W…w… what?" I stammered.

"I talked to Becky. You and she have discussed a great deal over the years, so she knew all about your past and relationships."

"How did you know where to contact her?"

"Mum had all the information in the detective's report. She gave it to me."

"That's a bit deceitful."

"Oh no, Jack. When a woman wants a man, she will do anything to get him. It's not deceitful, it's women's wiles. Anyway, Becky was quite happy to talk about you."

"Yeah, I bet."

"Jack. She is very fond of you. But after the way she behaved, twice I believe, she knows that you and she will never get any better than being friendly. She told me that if I get together with you, I will be a lucky woman."

At my age I shouldn't be surprised that women could be so devious. In fact every woman I have known had a little of that character. Having said that I still couldn't understand why someone as young and lovely as Ally wanted to hook up with a man my age. I need to make some things clear though. "Ally. Good as the thought is, I don't think we can ever be together." I was still sorting through my thoughts when tears started rolling down her cheeks. Difficult as it was, I had to ignore them. "You said yourself that my relationships have been long term, I am not Jack the Lad! If I found someone who would make me happy it would not be for the moment, or a couple of years. It would be for whatever remains of my life. I like you Ally, and I have no doubt that I would grow to love you. If I look into the future though, all I can see is despair when you have moved on to someone closer to your age. I heard what you said about age the other day, But you cannot pretend it isn't there. The older you get the more difficult it becomes to find love, and finding it with you would be a fool's paradise, if after a year or two I am alone again, as I most assuredly would be." I leant over and kissed her tears away. "You have paid an old man a great compliment. Please let me live with good memories, not hurt."

Ally threw her arms around me, holding me tight. "It wouldn't be like that. The more you say, the more I admire and respect you. The more I love you, Jack. I am not some silly girl, a butterfly flitting from one flower to another. I'm thirty five, Jack. I have done the dating scene, and the superficial men there, are not what I want. I want a man who recognises me as a person, a man who makes me feel warm and cared for. I would not want to go back to dross, when I have the real thing in my life." I heard her words and wanted so much to believe her. Yet my logic was telling me that loneliness and hurt were awaiting me after a year or two.

I got up, and reached for my jacket. "I'm sorry Ally. Very sorry. I believe that you believe what you are telling me, but I am the one who is fearful of the hurt that will inevitably happen. Call it self-preservation if you will, but I have to go with my instincts. Don't think badly of me, please."

I drove slowly and yes if you ask I did shed a tear. Who wouldn't? Back home I poured myself a glass of Bushmills malt whiskey. If ever there was a night that needed a drink, this was it. The ten year old malt warmed inside, as someone once said 'Like angels dancing on your tongue'; he had to have been Irish! The next couple of days were absolutely miserable, yet I was consoled by telling myself that this misery was still better than the misery that would descend on me when Ally eventually walked away from me. This I could cope with.

Two days later I had just finished on the treadmill, when the doorbell rang. It was Ally! "Morning Jack. I came for my workout." She blithely walked through to the conservatory as if nothing had happened. I was flabbergasted, standing there still holding open the door. Do I go and tell her straight away that she shouldn't be here? Do I go and shower and talk when she was done? From somewhere inside me a little chuckle rose, admiring her audacity. By God! This girl had balls! I went and showered, shaved and quickly got into slacks and a sweat shirt. I was sitting in the kitchen drinking tea when Ally came in to join me, a towel wrapped around her hair after her shower. I said nothing, as she helped herself to a mug of tea, then sat down opposite me. She smiled sweetly and blew me a kiss.

"Oh I need this tea, Jack." She sipped. "Oh I didn't thank you properly for the dance. Mum said she couldn't believe how good we looked together on the floor. Thank you for allowing me to share that with you."

"Ally! What are you doing here? I thought that the position was clear." She agreed with me.

"Yes, you made your position clear. I still have my thoughts on that subject, and nothing you said has changed my mind."

"Ally, let's not get into an argument."

"No. Let's not. But I will take up the point you made. That I would eventually tire of you and find someone else nearer my age. I can tell you until I am blue in the face that won't happen, but I can't prove it to you. So I decided that my actions will speak louder than my words. Jack you will see me here to exercise every other day without fail. If you don't let me in, I shall just wait on the doorstep until you take pity on me, and you will, Jack. I know you well enough to realise that. I will continue like that even if it takes two or three years to convince you. If that's what it takes then that's how long it will be, but I will convince you."

Oh shit, I thought, she is going to stalk me. I got up to make another pot of tea.

"Making another pot, Jack? I'll have one if you don't hate me already. Oh, and do you have any bread? I could make some toast for us." I opened the bread bin and indicated the toaster. Ally got on with that whilst I made the tea. Next she was opening the cupboards looking for and then finding the preserves.

"Jam or Marmalade? Jack."

"Marmalade please, Ally." By the time I had sat down with the two mugs of tea, she placed plates on the table with a dish of butter, and a dish of Marmalade. That's what women do. I would have put the butter on the table still in its packet, and knifed the marmalade straight from the jar.

"I prefer marmalade as well. Isn't that good?" There was a wealth of meaning in that little comment.

I had finished two slices of toast when she informed me of the rest of her plan.

"I want you to think about it. I will be here every other day as long as it takes for you to understand that I mean what I say. And I want you to know that every day of that time you will be denying both of us the pleasure of making love together." There were tears in her eyes now. "And I do so want to make love with you, Jack. But it will not happen until you tell me that you believe me. I will not be seeing anyone else, I only want you." I sat back in amazement, unable to offer any comment as her monologue went on. "You may ask me out for meals, or theatre and I will accept. You may take me back to my flat, and I will even ask you in. But at the end of the evening, Jack, I will retire to my chaste bed, and you will come home here to your cold bed, cold because I am not in it." She got out a tissue and wiped her eyes. "My father will eventually find out that we are not together, and he will be as pleased as Punch. That is not a reason for you to change your mind; I just pointed that out for you to think on." She thought for a moment. "Yes, I think I have covered everything. Oh yes! There is another thing." Her face softened. "I was so touched that you didn't mention my posing naked as a reason. For most men that would be the first thing they would say."

I thought that now was the time I could say something, before she started again. "I didn't mention it, because it was immaterial to my feelings. You did say that you would explain it when we are in bed together, well that may never happen, or it may be a year or two away."

"Well, when that happens, and it is a when, Jack, not if. Then I will explain. But I made my mind up, not to do anymore. It wouldn't be fair to my lover, or dare I say husband, to have photos of me naked turning up."

"Lover or husband eh? Is it one of each or are they one and the same?" I was laughing gently now, so that she would know that I was not being nasty. Ally grinned, accepting the Olive branch of humour.

"One and the same, and his name will be Jack Hunter. I want to be Mrs. Alicia Hunter and God help if you ever call me anything but Ally."

"You have it all worked out, don't you. Perhaps I should give up now and save you a lot of trouble."

Ally was not happy with that. "No, Jack. I have got to prove to you that I am sincere. I don't want you looking over your shoulder all the time wondering when it will happen. You have to know it won't, I have to prove to you that it won't."

"Twelve months." I said.

"What do you mean? Twelve months."

"That's what I will give you." Ally didn't understand what I was saying.

"You think that in twelve months I will give up?"

"No. Twelve months will give us ample time to really get to know each other. Time for both of us to make up our minds that we should be together, or go our separate ways. Twelve months. We will go out together. Dining, theatre as you suggested. I will give you a key for the house, so you can let yourself in, even if I'm away. You know bloody well I wouldn't leave you standing on the doorstep. I mean, what would the neighbours say?" Ally smiled at that. "If we are still together after twelve months, we will know if we have something going for us. Agreed?" Ally was nodding her head enthusiastically.

"Oh yes, Jack." She came round to my side of the table and kissed me, an open mouthed kiss of passion, flavoured with marmalade. She was all smiles. When she sat down again I saw the question come to her face.

"Why the change of heart?" I had expected that.

"It was something you said." I could see her going over her words trying to identify the content. "It was when you said you had made up your mind not to do anymore modelling. I didn't ask you to do that, it was your decision. That you could give up the work you do in order to save me embarrassment was very significant. In point of fact, if it was just glamour as you say, I don't think it would have been a problem for me."

"It wouldn't?"

"No. Ally you are the most beautiful woman I have ever known. If seeing your photos will give pleasure to others why not?"

"Thank you, compliments are always accepted." She paused. "But I have made up my mind. I want to be yours, Jack. And if this will help convince you, I am pleased that I made that decision."

"If you do stop modelling, what will you do for a living?"

"Oh, that's easy. I will go back to soliciting." She laughed happily at the shocked expression on my face. "Jack. I am a qualified Solicitor."

The rules had been set, and our lives intertwined. Ally would arrive every other day, letting herself in and getting on the rowing machine and then the treadmill, showering, and eventually joining me in the kitchen for tea and toast. She was quite nonchalant about walking around my home in her sweat-soaked Tee and shorts, she never wore a bra to exercise and her nipples were always very prominent. After eating she would get dressed and go to work. She kept some of her business suits in my closet. We went out to the Theatre in Derby, Concerts in Birmingham, and for dinner. Sometimes I would prepare dinner at my house, or she would prepare the same at her flat. Hugs and kisses were allowed, even passionate kisses, but nothing else. We exchanged emails regularly, and I even sent her some of the short stories I had written. These sparked some very long and in depth conversations. Some of my stories contained descriptions of sexual encounters. Ally enjoyed reading those.

"Your imagination is fantastic and the descriptions so vivid. When we are together, Jack, can we make love as your characters do? I get very warm when I read those, and very angry as well." She looked at me accusingly. "Because you are denying us all of that." I grinned.

"Ally, those passages are fantasy, not reality." She hit straight back with a play on my words.

"My passages are not fantasy, and I long for them to be filled by you, as your heroine have them filled." There was little I could say to that, as I was becoming eager to do with Ally that which my characters did in my stories.

This quasi affair was in its fifth month, and going well, when I had a visit from Sheila. She yet again thanked me for my help in getting Ewing back into line, then went on to congratulate me for getting Ally to stop modelling and back to the Law.

"It had nothing to do with me, Sheila. That was Ally's decision."

"Jack, it had everything to do with you!" I was surprised that Sheila knew about the modelling in the first place. Sheila told me that Ally didn't have secrets, although her father was kept in the dark. I could understand that.

"She also told me Jack, that you seemed to be OK with it if she had gone on. That's most generous of you."

"It wasn't an issue, Sheila. Ally made her choice, and whatever way it had gone I would respect her choice."

"As you say, Jack. Immaterial now. The only man she wants to be naked for now is you. But I have to say, that this twelve months understanding is good. It's making her think and work for what she wants. Not a bad idea in my book. But I can say one thing. She would never have left you."

I still had my thoughts on that. Admittedly not as definite as before, but still nagging away in my mind. "I'm not so sure about that, Sheila. She is so young and vibrant, so full of life. I am not certain that I can give her the exciting life she wants."

"Rubbish! I know my daughter. She is so much in love with you; she is worried silly that she won't be able to be the woman you need. Her worry is not that she will leave you, it's that you could leave her!" Now that was something I hadn't thought about. Sheila was smiling; she could read the thoughts going through my mind. Why do women always have to be so damned clever when it comes to relationships? "There is something else, Jack. Ally is putting in a lot of effort to reconcile with her father." Now that did shock me.

"Well I am pleased about that. But I have to say that Ally was really quite adamant that she wanted as little to do with him as possible. What brought this about?"

"In a word, Jack. You."

"Me?"

"Yes, you. Ally is preparing her father for the day she tells him that you and she are getting married." I laughed then.

"She is determined isn't she?"

"Oh yes. She was infatuated with you before the Ball, but after, when she realised that it wasn't going to be as easy as she thought, she re-assessed the relationship. Then you and she cooked up this twelve month idea, now, she has seen the qualities of Jack Hunter she didn't know about. Sorry, Jack, but you have a lovely young woman hopelessly in love with you." She looked to see how that affected me. "She doesn't want an affair, she doesn't want to be your live-in lover; she wants to be your wife, because that makes a statement of permanence."

"I don't stand a chance, do I Sheila?"

"No, Jack. But then, you never did."

CHAPTER SEVEN

A few weeks after my conversation with Sheila, I discovered a hotel near Chester that held residential weekend ballroom classes. Sometimes they were even hosted by a couple of the professionals on Strictly come Dancing. I mentioned this to Ally, wondering if she would like to go. "With you?"

I nodded. "Yes, with me."

"Separate rooms?"

"Yes. In keeping with our agreement, separate rooms."

Ally was thinking about that. "You're right; it has to be separate rooms, although I would wish otherwise. I made the rules so I have to keep to them. I would love to go, Jack."

"Then we shall go. I will make a booking."

The first weekend I could get a booking was three weeks away, and although the classes were being held by another professional couple, who did not appear in Strictly it was no matter. We drove up on the Friday evening and checked in, arranging to meet for dinner at eight o' clock. Even as we sat down to our meal, the orchestra was playing in the ballroom and Ally was impatient to get to the dance. That evening there was no tuition, so we were able to dance and enjoy ourselves. We changed partners for a couple of dances, something that Ally was concerned about. I explained that changing partners from time to time was important for developing our skills.

Saturday was all about tuition, with the professional dancers there from ten o' clock. They would demonstrate steps, and then allow the pupils to practice, incorporating the new steps in their routine. The professional dancers would wander around watching critically, and stepping in to demonstrate, also splitting a couple up and dancing with them separately for a few minutes. In the evening it was a grand Ball, Dinner jackets for the gentlemen and ball gowns for the ladies. Ally didn't wear her ball gown from before, and had opted for another in a very pale green, it covered her more completely, but the bodice was so tight it only served to accentuate her allure. Our dancing had affected

Ally as much as the first time we really danced together. There is something about the constant body contact and two bodies moving in unison that stirs the libido. We were on a large floor and the other dancers were just as proficient as us, therefore we could expand the envelope a little and dance the more complicated steps. Towards the end of the evening, we were dancing a very slow fox trot, ignoring the steps but basically hugging in time with the music.

"Jack. Could we suspend the agreement, just for tonight?" She raised her eyes to mine. "We don't have to make love, just sleep together. I want to go to sleep in the arms of the man I love, and wake up in the morning next to him. Please, Jack." Ally was trying to square the circle. I could not immediately give her an answer. We made our way back to the table and I was still in conflict. My deepest desire was to say yes, take this lovely woman back to her room and make love to her. That was my loins speaking, yet at the same time my logic was telling me that would be wrong. But it couldn't tell me how to explain that to Ally without making her feel rejected. I just opened my mouth and my heart, and hoped she would understand.

"Ally, if you could see inside my heart, you would know how much I am tempted. How much I want you. I am not being cold and heartless when I say that we cannot suspend our agreement. If we do it makes a nonsense of all that has happened over the last six months, why did we punish ourselves? Believe me it was painful, except to find out if we could commit to each other in time. Denying ourselves was part of the agreement, you said it, that you would go to your chaste bed, and I would go home to my cold bed. If we now say that for one night it suits us to ignore that, then the agreement is a mockery." She looked miserable hearing my words. "My sweet, Ally. You must have realised how my feelings have changed over the months. I know that not being able to see you often will leave a great aching chasm in my life. I enjoy your company more than ever, and my feelings towards you are growing warmer every day. Let's keep travelling this road, please?"

The look of misery was replaced with one of hope. "OK, Jack. I suppose you are right." We were walking towards the lift when she said. "I'm glad it has been painful for you." She grinned at me. "It means I am getting to you, Jack."

Was I right? I think so, much as I was coming to the conclusion that Ally would be steadfast, there was still that little Gremlin that reminded me that I could still be deserted at some time in the future.

We were travelling back the next day. Ally had been very thoughtful for most of the morning. I did wonder what that was about. She cleared the air when she turned in her seat. "Thank you, Jack." I may have looked surprised, wondering why she was thanking me. "You were right last night; our agreement has to be seen through to the end, whatever that may be. I was wrong, but you couldn't know, my Darling, how I wanted you. I was lying, when I said I wanted to go to sleep in your arms. I did but I wouldn't have let you sleep until you had made love to me." I was smiling then.

"Ally. There would have been no doubt about that."

She had a laugh in her voice. "Well, all you had to do was say yes." There was a moment of silence. "I called you darling, you didn't react to that." I shrugged my shoulders as well as you can when driving.

"I called you my sweet Ally, last night."

"I know. A girl remembers things like that and it thrilled me. Is it alright if I call you darling?"

"No problem."

"Good. I have wanted to call you that for a long time, you don't know how often it almost slipped out."

"Well it bloody well almost slipped in last night. More than once I almost got up and came to your room."

"No, no, Jack. Remember the agreement and my terms." I could hear in her voice the teasing tone. Then it changed. "If you had my Darling you would have discovered me doing something that may have got you really hot. My fingers were very busy." This conversation was getting too much for me.

"Let's talk about the weather. I really have to concentrate on driving."

Ally giggled, happily. "Yes perhaps that is best."

"Oh look!" I said. "The Sun's starting to shine."

Looking back on that weekend it proved that Ally and I were becoming more comfortable with each other, and with our sexuality. For me in particular I realised that I eagerly anticipated her joining me for workouts. It wasn't that I saw her in very skimpy clothing, although that was delightful, but our habit of sitting down afterwards and having breakfast. Ally knew her way around my kitchen well, and we worked as a team, our individual activity slotting seamlessly to produce the drink and food. Conversation was always bright, cheerful and interesting. She would tell me of her work; without mentioning names of course; and I would discuss the plot lines I was developing in my latest story, and listen carefully to her observations. Some of my stories had been published on the internet on free sites, and Ally brought up the topic of my being paid.

"I don't write to be paid. I enjoy the writing and the reward I get is the pleasure I can hopefully give to others by reading them."

"But what about your novel?" I had mentioned that to Ally some time ago, and she had read quite a lot of it. "You haven't done anything with that for some time."

"I'll get back to that soon, I promise. I know how the ending will be, it's just how to get there which is a problem at the moment."

"Will you put that on the internet?"

"No, Ally. If I think it good enough, I will find a Literary Agent to see if it can be published properly."

"See that you do. It's good, and I want to find out how it ends. And I will look after the contract for you."

"Solicitors are expensive aren't they?"

"I will do it at a special rate for you."

"And what sort of rate will that be? Forty quid an hour rather than sixty?"

"Oh no. It will be free. Well almost free." She giggled mischievously. "Payment in kind." I knew what she meant.

"Can I ask a question?"

"Yes." I wondered where she was going now.

There was a moment as she gathered her thoughts. "Your stories are all romances, with a bit of sex thrown in. I like the sex bits." She grinned inviting me to comment. "Are you writing from experience by any chance? You have main characters doing some quite inventive stuff. If you are, I have interesting and exciting times to look forward to." Ally's eyes sparkled. "But why romances?" I shrugged my shoulders.

"Boy meets girl, boy loses girl, boy finds girl again. They live happily ever after. It's the oldest plot in literature. You can add making love, tears, joy, anger and all sorts of emotions. There's all sorts of situations you can weave into that basic. Why do I write them? It makes me feel good, by writing them and hopefully others by reading them. I suppose I am a romantic at heart."

Ally was in complete agreement. "I know you are, Jack." Then the twinkle came to her eyes.

"Well, I like your descriptions of making love, and you can write about us when we have made love." Then she changed her mind about that. "But I don't think I want that being published."

It was getting close to Christmas, three months until our agreement was fulfilled. Ally had little choice but to go to her parents for Christmas, but she was adamant that it would only be for the day. Boxing Day she would be with me. For some years now the festival had not meant that much to me, so I had no problem being alone on Christmas Day, it was a day much like any other. Because Ally would be here on Boxing Day I had gone to some trouble, putting up an artificial tree with fibre-optic lights, and some multi-coloured flashing lights around the window. On the day I was settling down to watch the DVD of 'Dances with Wolves', a classic movie from my point of view, when the phone rang. I was very surprised when I recognised Richard Ewing's voice.

"Mr. Hunter, I am told that you have been seeing a lot of my daughter."

"That's correct, Mr. Ewing."

"I was once of the opinion that you were seeing her to interfere in my life. A sort of revenge for my interfering in yours." I said nothing as any confirmation may lead to the revelation of Sheila's involvement. My silence he could take as confirmation or not, but it did compel him to go on. "It would appear that Alicia has formed a strong regard for you. It would also appear that you have not taken advantage of that. I am grateful. But could I ask you what are your intentions towards my dau...." He stopped speaking suddenly. I heard Ally's voice in the background.

"Who are you talking to Daddy? Is it Jack? It is, isn't it? How dare you. It is nothing to do with you." I heard the phone rattle as if she was trying to wrestle the phone from Ewing, then after some muffled conversation she spoke to me.

"Jack! Is that you?"

"Happy Christmas, Ally."

"And Happy Christmas to you my Darling. What has my father been saying?"

"Not much, really. He is aware that we have been seeing each other, and he seems to be pleased that I haven't taken advantage of you. That hasn't happened without lots of cold showers I have to say. Oh and he wants to know my intentions, but I think you heard that bit."

"Yes I did. Well if that's all then he hasn't upset me. Has he upset you, though?"

"No. But I do understand now when you mentioned about his being over-protective, I mean you are over the age of consent aren't you. But fathers always have a care for their little girls, so don't blame him for that."

"Well if you say he didn't upset you, I will let him off. What are you doing today?"

"I was just sitting down to watch 'Dances with Wolves'"

"I have heard that's very good."

"It is. Tell you what, I will leave it now, and we can watch it tomorrow if you like."

"I like! Can we snuggle on the couch?"

"Yes."

"Well don't take a cold shower tomorrow." She giggled.

"I hope your father can't hear you."

"Oh yes. He's still in the room."

"Ally! You can be a bitch at times can't you?"

She laughed. "Yes, Darling I can. See you tomorrow at workout time."

"OK my Love, see you then."

Ally came in at her usual seven-thirty and found me on the treadmill, I was a little late. She waited until I had warmed-down and stopped then grabbed me and kissed like it was the last kiss she would ever give. I was breathless already, and after that kiss I needed another, the kiss of life! She had the biggest smile on her face. "Phew! I am not complaining, but what was that about?"

"You called me my Love yesterday."

"Did I? I must have forgotten."

"Oh no you haven't. I know you now, Jack Hunter, and you don't do things like that unless you mean them, nor forget either." I smiled.

"Perhaps it just slipped out."

"Oh no. Any way you prefer slipping in." There was a smile of invitation on her lips. I kissed her. I pointed to the Rowing machine.

"Workout! And get rid of your excess energy. Today is a day of relaxing, doing nothing. We'll eat, drink, and then play couch potatoes in front of the telly. Suit you?"

"As long as your arms are round me, definitely."

Our breakfast went as usual. I had hardly noticed over these months that our closeness and comfort being with each other had increased exponentially. With simple tasks like preparing food, eating together, then washing up the dishes we had developed an easy division of labour that required no thought. Our bodies touched as a matter of course doing these jobs and we had long got out of the need for an apology, indeed the touches were a source of pleasure in the intimacy. Together we prepared a light salad lunch keeping it in the fridge so that it could be served whenever we were ready to eat. I had a jug of soup, ready to heat in the micro wave.

Ally had printed off one of my stories, one in which an older man and a younger woman find love together. It was one of a number she could have picked, so I suspected an ulterior motive in her choosing this one. We read it together and she would ask me about the motivation behind various episodes. When their first sex scene came up, she read it aloud, but with a blush on her face that had me chuckling inwardly. Having finished the scene she looked at me shyly.

"Is that how it will be for us?"

"Is that how you want it to be?" Funnily we neither questioned that we would make love together, it had gone from 'if' to 'when'.

She nodded. "Yes. I want it to be as gentle, as loving and caring as that."

"Do you think it could any other way than that?" Ally shook her head.

"Not with you, my Darling."

She read on, and then got her Solicitor's hat on. "You rationalise the age difference here quite well, in fact from her point of view the relationship can work well. So why did you make such a point about the difference in our ages?"

I had thought this would come up when Ally picked this story out. "If you read it properly, not just picking out the facts that aid your argument, you will see that James is challenging Elaine to think clearly about the consequences. I was attempting to make you think through that problem as well. In fact this whole twelve month thing should be making you concentrate on that. It should have given you an insight into Spring and Autumn relationships, and whether you will want a man closer to your own age." I paused and another fact came to me. "However close the relationship is, there is an imbalance, and eventually that imbalance will show up."

"You really don't get it, do you? Jack. Your writing suggests you understand women, but you don't. A woman doesn't make a logical and considered choice about who she falls in love with, she just falls in love. And nothing can change that. He may be unsuitable, it doesn't matter she's in love with him. He may be a brute, it doesn't matter she's in love with him. He may be ugly, it doesn't matter she's in love with him. And he may be older by twenty years, it doesn't matter she's in love with him." Ally's emotion had her breathing hard and fast. "I am in love with you, Jack. Perhaps it was infatuation when we started this, but over these months I have fallen, fallen so deeply in love with you. I want to be with you always, I want to sleep next to you every night, I want to be your wife and give you a child. That's how it is when a woman's in love. The obstacles mean nothing; all that matters is her emotions." There were tears in her eyes as she made her impassioned declaration. I couldn't sit there and not react. Men did perhaps get too logical, making factual decisions in spite of their gut feelings. I got up and fetched a tissue. After she had dried her eyes I held her close.

"Ally, my dear, adorable, sweet Ally. Every time I put obstacles in the way, I was tearing myself apart inside. When I left your flat after the Ball, I don't quite know how I managed to get home. I couldn't see clearly because I was crying. I had just told a most beautiful woman that I wouldn't have a relationship with her. That was self-inflicted pain. Thank you for not giving up on me. I don't deserve you, but I am not about to let you go, nor put obstacles in the way anymore. I love you Ally." I felt her quiver.

"You do?"

"Yes. I love you."

"What about the twelve months?"

"In three weeks it will be twelve months since we met, will that do?" She gave that thought.

"Bugger twelve months!"

"That's what I think too. Bugger twelve months." She raised her head to look at me; the tears were back in her eyes. I kissed them away.

"Am I staying tonight?"

"Yes."

"Will you say it again, please, Jack." I knew what she meant.

"My beautiful, adorable, Ally. I love you." Her smile put the Christmas lights to shame.

With so much emotion between us, it seemed sensible to just relax together and enjoy 'Dances with Wolves'. We cuddled on the couch. Ally snuggling under the arm I had put around her shoulders, her legs across my lap. From time to time she would raise her lips to mine, and our tongues would gently caress together. I could now allow myself a little exploration, and my hand cupped her breast over her sweat top, A little later, Ally took my hand and moved it under the sweater and moved it toward her breasts. She moved slightly giving me access. I already knew she wasn't wearing a bra, yet it was still a surprise when my fingers found, touched and captured her nipple. A sharp intake of breath told me that the sensation was just as exhilarating for her as for me.

"I have lain awake at nights, wondering how your hand on my breasts would feel. I never thought it would be this good though." She murmured. "Don't forget I have two." We slouched as before watching the film, my fingers almost absent-mindedly playing over her nipples alternately. Engrossed in the film, time slipped away unnoticed, the last scene and after word, describing how the culture of the Plains Indians was destroyed brought to us a sense of poignancy. It upset Ally and she held me tight, lifting her lips searching for mine to join her in a kiss.

The light was fading fast, and I drew the curtains and considered switching on an additional table lamp before deciding that the lights from the Christmas tree and the one table lamp was sufficient, the illumination in the room was soft and gentle. It was warm, private and ours for as long as we wished. Taking my place on the couch, Ally immediately came into my arms again demanding a kiss. I slipped her sweater up, exposing her breasts and lowered my head to take one nipple after the other into my mouth, sucking, tonguing, and biting them gently. Ally's moans and sharp intake of breath told me that she was enjoying my ministration.

"Oh Jack. That is so, so good." She wriggled, trying not to dislodge my mouth, as she drew her sweater over her head. Casting it casually to one side, she lay back, and drew my head back to her breasts. I resisted for a moment, as this was the first time I had actually seen them properly. She looked at me as I looked at her breasts.

"Do you like them, Jack?"

"Your breasts are beautiful, Ally. I love them as I love you."

She smiled tenderly. "They are yours. Take them please."

I had written about two people making love in my stories, but knew that I could never describe this. It was beyond words, our loving lay somewhere in an astral plane, where bodies as such didn't exist. Where our two spirits became one in a dance as old as time. When did Ally divest herself of her clothes to lay naked on the couch, calling for me to join her and join with her? When did I discover that I too was without clothes, not remembering how and when I had, or perhaps we, had taken them off. Nothing mattered, the world outside had little meaning, there was just us. Ally gasping as I sucked and licked her emissions of love direct from the fount, the scream as she came, her sibilant triumphant "yes" simultaneous with my gasp as I entered her for the first time, the cries of delight, the moans of passion, Ally's wail and my howl as our orgasms charged like electricity through our bodies, the long drawn out "no", as I slipped shrivelling from her body, and the sound of her sucks as she cleansed my cock of our combined juices followed by the kiss I claimed immediately after. Sounds and sensations almost impossible to describe, yet with a meaning known to us both that told a story far more powerful than mere description of our acts.

We clung together our drying liquids slick on thighs and bellies, without words. An occasional shiver, a quiver, out of nowhere, claiming our bodies, engendering in the other a similar response. Slowly, gradually heart beats and breathing returned to normal, and the cuddle became one of deep empathy as passion receded. A little voice murmured against my chest.

"Your writing didn't prepare me for that."

I shook my head even though Ally couldn't see that. "I am not good enough to write a description of those feelings. That was beyond my imagination."

I felt her nod then raise her face. Tears had streaked her cheeks. "Wherever I was, my Love, my Darling man. I have never been there before."

"Neither have I, Ally. Neither have I!"

CHAPTER 8

The house was warm; we had privacy so felt no need to dress again. Ally wore a cheeky grin as we made drinks and a snack. She took to caressing my bottom at every opportunity, explaining.

"It's nice to see a man who doesn't have a hang up about being nude. Men seem to think that women don't have an interest in seeing their lover naked. They do and I love this." And she caressed my bottom once again, and then gave me a light smack. "I could get you some commissions to pose you know." Now she was going too far. I laughed.

"I doubt that the people who bought your photos would be interested in a fifty five year old man." Ally had this big grin.

"Possibly not, but the gay trade would love you!" Laughing hilariously she dashed out of the kitchen before I could catch her.

It was getting late when Ally explained a little about her modelling career.

"I never posed with a man, you know." She seemed desperate to re-assure me on that. Now up to that point I had given no thought to the possibility she could have posed with anyone else. She turned in my arms to look me in the eyes. "No lies though, Jack. I did pose with other girls some times." She waited for my reaction.

"I assume there was a good artistic reason." She shook her head.

"No, there was a good commercial reason. Lesbian portrayals sell. Jack, I am not a lesbian. We posed to suggest that lesbian activity was taking place, it was always soft core, we didn't do hard. You don't have to, but I would like to show you some of the photos soon. I want to get this out of our way."

I wasn't sure that I wanted to see the pictures, after all it was Ally in the pictures, but like most men I was drawn to any depiction of the naked female form. "Let's see about that. It's not important to me and we'll talk some other time. Ally. I know you are worried about this, but I really don't have a problem. How can I explain it? Yes! I know. Neither of us are virgins. What we have done before, who we have slept with is in the past, it makes no difference to who we are now and the feelings we have for each other. The only important fact is that we are together; the past is white-washed, history. The future is what matters."

Ally was quiet as she thought about what I had said. "I understand what you are saying, Jack. But there are pictures of my past, they could emerge and I don't want them to come between us."

"They won't, my Darling, it is not important, but right now, Ally, what is important is that I take you to bed and make love to you." Her eyes softened and her worried expression was replaced with desire. She understood now that what she had done was not important, in the same way that the men previously in her life were unimportant to me. She was here with me now.

"My lovely man. How many times will you remind me how right I was to fall in love with you? Yes, Darling, take me to bed and make me your woman. Erase the past."

I had this exquisite woman in bed with me. She lay naked allowing me to explore with my eyes, my hands, and my tongue. I did all of these, and was so captivated by her beauty I could not hurry, taking time to worship every part of her in depth. Ally at first seemed to be impatient, then acquiescent, then trancelike as waves of pleasure rolled through her. When I finally I moved over her body, she opened her legs happily to accept me, calling me to invade her body, to take her and allow her to become my woman. The warmth and wetness that welcomed me was overwhelming, I tried so hard to last, biting my lip hoping that the pain would delay me, it did but only momentarily. The roller that started life as a small ripple far out to sea approached the shore, building in height, and as it built the seas around it were disrupted by its passing, then it towered, tall and strong, until finally the base was insufficient to support the crest and it crashed, turbulent, without control. I was dimly aware that as I came, Ally screamed and came as well, joining me in that tumbling chaos of wave and currents.

Awaking in the morning I was a little bewildered. After so many months of sleeping alone, there was a warm body next to mine. I opened my eyes to see her two brown eyes, swimming with love watching me. I smiled in response to Ally's smile. "Good morning Darling."

"Good morning to you as well my Darling." I replied. "Did you sleep well?"

"I had a lovely night, Jack. I was sleeping next to my man, and I awoke beside him. I have been watching you for some time, trying to convince myself that this is true. It ought to be a dream. My man made love to me last night, I had never thought it could be so overwhelming and beautiful, but it was, and I slept in his arms. I want nothing else in my life except to love you and be loved by you."

"Nothing else?" I queried.

"Well perhaps one thing else."

"What would that be?"

"I want to give you a child! Please Jack. Our baby." She blushed; very prettily I have to say.

Now I already had a daughter, Libby. Who I saw rarely, and those meetings were fraught with bitterness. In the divorce her mother got custody, and I had visiting rights, but as usual in these cases, my ex-wife managed to put all sorts of obstacles in the way of my visits. Little obstacles like moving, and not letting me know where she had gone to, and using a solicitor who obviously had a grudge against cheating husbands and would take so long to reply to letters from my solicitor, that any information grudgingly passed on was out of date within a week. Then the whole cycle would start again. I thought that it would change when my ex-wife died of Liver and Kidney failure, but my daughter who was twelve at the time was placed in foster care. Social services did not believe that a single man, me, even though I was her father, was suitable to bring up a child. When Libby was eighteen, she contacted my solicitor and got my address and phone number. We spoke and met, but after so long a time it was difficult to re-establish any kind of relationship. Her mother had told her that I wanted nothing to do with her at all and the years of brain-washing had taken their toll. You cannot reverse that in five minutes. We did see each other from time to time and gradually started to forge some kind of friendship.

I would be very happy to have a child with Ally. My reasoning was that at some time in the future when I was dead, she would not be left completely alone. Another other reason my cynical mind came up with was that it would tie us closer together. Again as I had seemingly lost a daughter there would be a child for me to love. The overwhelming reason though was simple; the child would be our child, born of our love.

"Well there are two things that need to happen before that." I got up on my knees. "Dear, sweet Ally. I love you and want you in my life always. Will you marry me?" Ally collapsed in irrepressible laughter at the sight, me naked, on my knees, swaying unsteadily on the bed, proposing marriage. Undaunted I went on. "And if you say yes then the second factor is you coming off the pill."

"We don't have to get married." Ally replied through her laughter.

"Oh yes we do." I was adamant. "No child of mine will be born illegitimate."

"In that case." Ally got on her knees to face me, equally naked. "I willingly accept your proposal." She giggled with mirth. "I want to be Mrs. Jack Hunter. We don't have to worry about the pill, I am not taking it so we may have started the baby already, but in case we haven't, my Darling lover, we will have to do a lot more of this." She demonstrated her intention by reaching down and taking hold of a prominence, which she fondled. I was already erect, and Ally lay back pulling me by my erection.

"Time to start making a baby, Stud. I am in the middle of my cycle, and for you, lovely man, I am hot!" I was ready and Ally was soaking wet, so without any kind of foreplay I entered her warmth. She cried and shook her head from side to side.

"Oh God! Jack. I love that feeling as you slide in and fill me. Now have me. Give me your baby!" I think I may have done just that.

My being divorced meant it would not be possible to get married in Church. Ally had no problem with that, but Richard Ewing did. For one he was not happy about me as the intended husband, and if his daughter would not listen to reason and determined to marry me, it had to be in Church and a big production number befitting his position in the community. Ally eventually told him he had a choice, either accept our plans or she would cut him out of her life. With both Ally and Sheila bending his ear all the time, he did what any man would do, he caved in. Anything to keep the ladies sweet. I wanted Libby there of course, and invited her to visit and meet Ally. I think she was diffident about meeting Ally but eventually agreed. That visit was the one that blew the door off its hinges.

Libby had told me she would arrive in the afternoon. Ally was working so wouldn't get there until five thirty. I was pleased to see my daughter when she arrived. I thought I may have done something right, as Libby was a lovely young woman of twenty-three. Father's don't really look at their daughter's figures, but if I were a young man unrelated, I would certainly make a play for her. At first my daughter was defensive, she was still carrying the remnants of the brain washing, and her anger showed when she suddenly accused me of deserting her and not caring about her at all. I was taken aback by this attack. I could explain the situation forever but doubted that she would believe me, so I went up to my files and pulled the folder with all the solicitors' correspondence.

"Read this." I demanded, leaving her alone for a while. I made some tea, and sat unhappily in the kitchen wondering if I would ever get my daughter back.

She came to find me, tears running down her cheeks. "Daddy. I didn't know."

"I thought that was the case." I found her a box of tissues.

"Mummy made me believe that you wanted nothing to do with me. She said you didn't want to see me, that you didn't love me. Over the years she said you never paid for any support. It was all lies; she lied to me, all those years, she lied to me." I held her as she sobbed, trying hard not to feel bitter about it. "When mum died, they asked me if I wanted to live with you, but I didn't think for one moment you would want me." Her tears renewed. Eventually she regained her composure and I poured her some tea.

"Libby. I hurt your mum a great deal. You must understand that when someone is hurt that badly, they will try to get some kind of revenge. The only way your mother could do that was denying me the chance to watch you grow up, to be involved in your life. Don't hate her memory, because she loved you very much. It was the alcohol that clouded her judgement."

We talked for some time about all of this, the correspondence was enough for her to realise that I had not willingly stayed away from her, and I had pushed my solicitor down every avenue to get me the chance of visiting. She now knew that my support cheque was delivered promptly every month, and cashed. Now my task was to convince her not to hate her mother. As the afternoon wore on we were able to relax a little and even smile at some of the good memories. She asked about Ally. Libby didn't seem shocked at the difference in our ages, women seem to accept these things, whereas men would be nudging each other and cracking jokes about dying on the job, albeit with a smile on the face. I had been nervous about this meeting, but as time went on and Libby's attitude changed the nerves dissipated.

The key in the door alerted me to Ally's arrival.

"In the lounge." I called and Ally came through with a smile on her face. The smile was replaced by horror.

"Shit! Sacha." That was Ally.

"Belle! Oh bugger." That was Libby. I had got to my feet when Ally came in the room, now I stood frozen, trying to understand what had happened. They were both talking, confused words, disjointed sentences, neither making sense to me although they may have understood. Suddenly Libby had picked up her bag, and was walking towards the door. I raised my voice.

"Libby! Stay where you are and can we have quiet, please." They stopped and looked at me.

"Now will one of you, just one please, tell me what's going on here, and who the hell are Sacha and Belle?" They looked at each other guiltily it would be the bravest of the two who answered.

Eventually Ally elected to speak. "You remember when I was telling you about the photo shoots, that I would sometimes pose with some other girls?"

"Yes, I remember." I knew what she was going to say next. I looked at Libby as I said. "You are going to tell me that Libby was one of the models." Libby looked shamefaced.

"Well, Sacha er... Yes, she was. Jack. I had no idea she could be she your daughter, her name wasn't Hunter." My wife had reverted to her maiden name after the divorce and Libby obviously had used that name.

"I see."

Libby was crying. "Dad! I am so sorry. No one was ever meant to know."

I reached out and brought her into my arms to cuddle. "Libby. Why are you sorry? Did you happen to hear what Ally said? Did you not hear Ally say that she has already told me all about her modelling, and what style of modelling she did? Does it look as if I am angry with her? You can see that we are still together, and getting married, so what does that tell you?"

She wiped her eyes although still blubbering. "That you are OK with it?" Her voice contained hope.

"Yes. And if I am OK with my fiancé having done that, do you suppose that I would apply a different standard to my daughter?"

"I don't know."

Ally stepped in. "Sa…Libby. Your dad is a very understanding man. One of the reasons why I love him so much. I didn't want any secrets, so I told him all about the shoots, although he hasn't seen any of the photos."

I interjected. "I don't think I want to now."

"Jack! Be quiet." That was the first time Ally had spoken to me sharply. "Libby, I probably know your dad better than you do, I know you have had very little contact over the years, so I can tell you, he doesn't condemn me, and he won't condemn you either. He's not that sort of man." Libby looked apprehensively at me.

"Are you sure?"

"Would I be cuddling you like this if I wasn't?"

"I don't know. I haven't had a cuddle from my dad in twenty years."

I smiled. "Well if we can see each other often, then the cuddles will be often as well." Libby smiled.

"I would like that, Dad."

Ally and Libby went off to repair their faces, as Ally had an emotional moment when she understood that my daughter was back in my life. I had to wipe my eye; I think I got some grit in it. Then my thoughts turned to more mundane things. I had intended to cook, but decided that probably I would get a Chinese meal delivered. I wasn't going to go through that routine of giving them a choice; experience told me that by the time they had decided, I could have cooked a three course meal. So I just phoned the local restaurant and ordered a banquet for three. There would be enough choice there to satisfy both of them.

We were sitting eating when Libby challenged me. "Why don't you want to see some of the photos? Don't you think I am pretty enough?" I put my fork down; I could never pick enough up with chopsticks.

"Libby. You're my daughter. I shouldn't be looking at pictures of you in the nude."

"Why not? You saw me naked enough times when I was young."

"You were a baby then, it was different."

"So, if we had stayed together as a family, and went on holiday to the Med. I would probably have gone topless. You wouldn't have made a fuss about that, would you? You would have seen my tits. Or would you have averted your eyes?"

"What's this about, Libby? Are you in training to become a Lawyer by any chance?" Ally was grinning from ear to ear.

"She's doing well, Jack. Perhaps she ought to be."

"Dad. I am not ashamed of what I did. The photos were very good, and I earned good money for doing them. Belle…I mean Ally, says that you don't think there is anything wrong about posing so why not see them? I have no problem, Ally has no problem. What's your difficulty?"

Now when a man and a woman argue, the woman usually wins, because they cheat by making it emotional rather than logical. Now I had two women to argue with. There was no point in even trying. I threw in the towel. "OK, OK you win. I'll look." Don't you hate it when a woman smiles that little smile of victory? I looked from one to the other and both had that little smile. It did alleviate one problem I had considered, that Ally and Libby might not get on. The problem now was that I was certain they would get on so well that they could collaborate against me. Oh well! Winners can be losers at one and the same time. Ally decided to strike while the iron was hot, jumping up and running to get her lap-top from her car. I sat, my trepidation having ruined any appetite I may have had. Libby went round and conferred with Ally as to what pictures they would show me. Snippets of their discussion intriguing me.

"No, not that one, I look terrible in that."

"Yes, that's good."

"What do you think about that?"

"Umm well sort of. Now that one's better!"

They finally finished their selection and moved round, putting the lap-top in front of me and bringing their chairs round to sit either side of me. At first they only showed me pure glamour, bikinis were worn, and they were solo. Then tops came off, and the two were posing suggestively together. I was afraid as I waited for the first totally nude shots. When it hit the screen I was hyperventilating. It goes without saying that they were both lovely women. I could also see that they were both shaved, although there was nothing explicit with the poses, and they were very artistic. Ally softly asked.

"Well?"

"I don't know what to say. I suppose my imagination conjured images that were more...more revealing. You are both very beautiful, and the photos are erotic, sensual and artistic." I turned to Libby. "I am so happy to have a daughter who is so beautiful. Now I have two beautiful women in my life. It can't get better than that." Her face softened and a small smile graced her lips.

"Thank you, Daddy." Then I got mischievous.

"Great tits, Libby." Libby looked shocked for a second then as Ally collapsed into laughter, she saw the joke.

They showed me few more pictures, until right at the end one photo was displayed, and I loved it. They were standing close, both naked. Ally had her arm around Libby's shoulders as Libby appeared to cup and caress one of Ally's breasts. Together they looked down at where Libby's hand was. Ally's long blonde hair cascaded over one of her shoulders, highlighting the curve of her arm. I looked at this photo for quite some time. "It's beautiful."

Ally hugged my arm. "I thought you would like that one." Libby had said little, but I could hear her breathing short and fast.

"Could I have that enlarged? I would like to frame it, it's so lovely. My two lovely ladies together." Ally was smiling, and Libby looked as if all her ships had come home together. I put my arm round her.

"I never forgot you, and always hoped that someday I would have my daughter back. To find that she is such a lovely woman makes all the heartache seem worthwhile."

Ally had rested her head on my shoulder as we were looking at the slide show. When I made the comment about the last photo she kissed my cheek.

"It is a good shot. We can have it by our bed, can't we, Jack?" I pulled her leg a little.

"Well I don't know about that. It wouldn't be seemly to have my daughter watching us as we made love."

"Oh I think it would." Libby interrupted. "In fact I think I would rather like to watch. I could give scores, you know, six out of ten." The little tease was getting revenge.

"No. Libby." Ally retorted. "It would be ten out of ten, I can vouch for that." I knew this would happen. My two ladies were ganging up on me already.

We cleared away the dishes, putting the uneaten food into a Pyrex dish. That could be micro waved later. Ally got serious as we sat in the lounge with coffee.

"I think this is the time, Jack. To tell you more about the modelling, especially as Libby's here." Libby was nodding her head in agreement.

I groaned. "Do we have to?"

"Yes, Darling. I think so."

CHAPTER NINE

Ally started her story. "I don't know why, but six years ago I was really pissed off with my father, and wanted to do something shocking which would upset him. Stupid really, as he could never know what I did, but in my mind I was getting back at him. I had seen this advert asking for potential models, so I answered it. Thoughts of walking down the catwalk in all sorts of glamorous dresses filled my mind, but it wasn't that at all. They were looking for girls who would do nude modelling for photographers. It didn't take me long to sign on, after all it would be perfect for what I wanted. I soon found out that the modelling I was prepared to do was not the best paid, in fact if I agreed to doing sex acts for the camera with men and other women I could get anything up to four or five hundred quid for a day's work, cash!" She paused to drink some coffee, looking over the rim of the cup cautiously to see how I was reacting. "I didn't do any of that, Jack."

"I know. You told me, Ally."

"But I did do nude glamour. Nothing explicit though. And I could get something like a hundred to a hundred and fifty a day. After a while I realised that the photographer, once I had signed the model release, could get getting close to a thousand quid, selling sets of photos to various top shelf magazines, and I had no say in where it went. That's when I decided that if I was doing this I should get more for it, and moreover control where the photos were sold and to whom. I did some research and found that the States was the biggest market, and for some reason they liked English girls. I don't know why, as having seen some of their girls, they are absolutely knock-outs." I had some ideas of why this should be, but kept quiet; I didn't want to go off at a tangent. Ally waited for a moment, still unsure of my reaction, but as I said nothing, she carried on.

"That's when I decided that I would become a producer. I hired a studio, a photographer, and models. I had learned that Lesbian stuff sold well, so that's what I did. Some of the girls I booked were bi-sexual, and would happily get it on with other girls; I didn't pose in any of those sets. But I also found out that there were magazines and web-sites that wanted more artistic stuff, erotic rather than pornographic. I would do the artistic modelling. A suggestion that sex was going to happen. That's all. But if any of the girls didn't want publication in this country, their wishes were respected." I nodded.

"I can understand that, well actually you proved it to me with those photos. Two very beautiful girls appearing to show love for one another. Much more simulating then the explicit stuff. It appeals to the mind, and conjures a story." The photographer is good; he really captures your beauty.

Ally was smiling happily as she turned to Libby. "See! I knew it. Your dad looks beyond the obvious and sees the poetry." Libby was smiling as well, but it would seem for a different reason.

"Dad said I was a very beautiful girl." She was delighted.

However I had a question. "I think your policy of not publishing in this country was commendable. But! Surely if product went on the internet you had no control over who saw it and where." Ally agreed with that.

"Yes. But I made certain that none of the pictures appeared on free sites. If anyone had paid money to see the photos, then they were unlikely to publish the fact by 'outing' one of the girls. I was actually thinking about building my own site. But that won't happen now. You mentioned the photographer. Yes, Arnold is good, but he would be happier taking your pics, Jack, than ours." She was smiling mischievously.

"Gay?" I asked.

"Like a nine bob note."

Libby needed to tell me her side, although I could probably guess most of it. The tale was simple. She answered an advert, actually one placed by Ally, and decided once the whole thing was explained to her that she would do it.

"But Dad. It wasn't seedy or dirty. It was good to be posing with other girls, especially Ally, but most of all they thought I was lovely, and I needed to know that. I didn't mind posing in the nude, after all it's only a body and fifty percent of the world's population has the same body." Possibly I thought, but few as lovely as Ally and Libby. I suspected that she had an image problem though, and I had to feel some of the guilt for her low self-esteem. Could it be that my supposed rejection of her had planted the seed of self-doubt in her?

Libby seemed to be building up to something. She took a deep breath as if she had come to a decision. "I have to tell you, Dad. I am a lesbian!"

"So?"

Libby looked shocked as Ally burst into giggles. "I said, Dad that I was a lesbian."

"I heard you." I smiled at her. "Libby it doesn't matter who you love, man or woman. All that matters is that you have it in your heart to love someone."

Libby looked to Ally for help. "I knew, Libby." Ally said. "I'm with your dad on this. It doesn't matter who you love as long as you can love. We all need love."

My daughter got up and came round to where I was sitting. She knelt and hugged me. "I know you love me, Daddy, and I will try not to hate mum for keeping you away from me."

Our conversation had gone on long into the night, and I was not keen on Libby driving for a couple of hours that night. "There's a spare bedroom. Would you like to stay the night? Save you driving all that way at this time of night." Libby didn't think long.

"Thanks Dad, I would like that." Then a grin split her face. "As long as you two don't get it on and keep me awake. Ally laughed at my face which had gone bright red.

"It's OK, Libby. I'll give him a night off." Then Libby threw in the punch line.

"Unless I can come and watch!"

"Libby! This is your father talking. Go to bed."

"Yes. Daddy." She said this meekly, but had a smile on her face as she did.

In the morning there were three of us to work out. I was first, and then Ally and Libby worked together, one on the rowing machine the other on the treadmill, then swapping. Eventually I was presented with not one sweating girl but two, both of whom disdained a bra and both of whom had prominent nipples showing through the wet Tee's. I was sitting in the kitchen with my mug of tea when they came in, and much as I tried I could not look at Libby in that condition. She noticed and said to Ally.

"Even though he's seen the photos my dad doesn't think I have tits." Ally sympathised.

"Yeah, I know. He wouldn't look at mine for a long time. I made a point." She grinned. "Well actually two points of giving him every opportunity to look, but he wouldn't. Give him time, Libby, he'll get used to it. He'll have to." I had become used to Ally's expressions and tone as she said something, and there was a world of meaning in that comment. I left it for a while, hoping that Ally would think it had gone over my head.

When Ally got up to make some more toast that I casually asked. "Why should I have to get used to what?" For a moment neither could remember the context of the comment. Then Ally understood.

"Oh. I didn't think you had heard that." I smiled easily at my wife to be.

"No secrets? I thought that was the plan." She nodded. Then took a deep breath.

"As I have to all intents and purposes moved in here. I thought that rather than sell the flat, I would rent it. Libby asked if she could take the tenancy." I grinned.

"That is an excellent idea. It means that I will see more of my daughter, and also that you have a place to run to when I kick you out! As I most certainly will if you two connive without me." Ally was shocked that I could even think of that, and I grinned to show her I was joking. "If you have ideas, let's talk them through together. You never know I may be quite in favour. The calendar may say it, but I not too old to be reasonable." Libby looked ashamed and guilty, not so Ally, she had a grin on her face. All she said was,

"Don't worry, Libby. I know the best place to negotiate with your dad. And he is never old there!"

I turned to Libby. "And I suppose that you thought that you could carry on the business that Ally set up?" They both looked totally surprised.

"Were you listening to us?" Ally accused me.

"No, why? When did you discuss it?"

"I just mentioned it to Libby when we were exercising."

"Well I was having a shower then, and you know you can't hear anything over the noise of the water. It would appear that my mind was working the same way as you two. If Libby wants to continue, it seems the sensible solution."

"You don't mind, dad?" Libby was surprised as my attitude.

"No. I have learned enough about the profession from Ally and how you can be in control of the whole thing. Just don't do anything that will compromise your integrity. "Libby ran round the table and hugged me.

"You are the greatest dad. I will be living nearby, and we can make up for the years we didn't see each other." Then in the same breath.

"And I could I come over and work out regularly?" I nodded in resignation. My life now would be controlled by these two. Ally was happy. Then decided that she would add to the good feelings.

"I suppose that neither of you will be really interested in my news." That stopped everything.

"News?"

"Yes. I'm pregnant!"

"You're not?" I questioned.

"I am." Ally said proudly.

"When?"

"In seven months."

"Why didn't you tell me before?"

"I only got the confirmation yesterday, and I didn't think it would have been the right time to say anything last night, given the shocks we all had."

Suddenly I noticed Libby; she was sitting quietly and crying her eyes out. Concerned I put my arm round her.

"What's the matter, Libby?" She didn't answer at first and I got even more concerned.

Ally whispered to me. "She's happy, not sad."

Libby nodded. "I am happy dad. I haven't had a family for years. Now all of a sudden I have my Dad back, a step-mother who is more like a sister, and soon I will have a baby brother or sister. That's why I'm crying, I'm so happy." I will never understand women. Then I realised that I was in a similar position. I was getting a family too, something that

I had given up as impossible years ago. If I wasn't a bloke I would have been crying as well.

Libby continued to come and exercise every couple of days or so, and would come into the kitchen for a tea before going to shower. Her breasts were prominent in the sweat-soaked Tee, and it felt weird looking at her in that condition. Eventually Libby had enough.

"Dad. I am not trying to seduce you. I'm your daughter for God's sake. I don't wear a bra when training, it's too bloody uncomfortable. But you won't look at me when we are talking. I know now you didn't reject me when you and Mum split up, but not looking at me does feel like a kind of rejection. I can't help having breasts; they come with being a woman. Please don't avoid me." She was right and I felt so guilty. Ally watched me understanding the conflict in my head. She put her hand on mine. She didn't say anything, but her touch allowed me to resolve my problem.

"I am sorry, Libby. You are right. If we had been a proper family all those years, I would view you as a daughter first, woman second. All that time apart means we have lost a vital part of our connection. All I see is a lovely, young woman first, daughter second. I will try, Libby. I will try."

A week later they put me to the test. Ally remarked that she thought Libby's breasts were getting bigger.

"Do you think so?" Libby queried, lifting her top to expose herself and looking down at them.

"Pretty sure." Ally answered. "What do you think, Jack?" Well I looked, and then I motioned to Libby to turn sideways and looked some more.

"No, not really. I think it is the fact that she had got trimmer with all the exercise, just makes them look bigger." I think I passed the test, by the smiles on both their faces. I waited for a minute then looked at Libby.

"Satisfied, now?" She grinned. Then I renewed the comment of a week or so before.

"Great tits though!"

Ally and I got married a month later. There was no way we would be able to kid her parents that the baby had not been conceived before the wedding, we didn't even try. Ally told Sheila within two days of her telling me. We married in the Registry Office, much to Richard Ewing's displeasure. The man spoke to me as little as possible, but I gathered that he was under no illusions from Sheila that any sign of petulance or threats would result in the boom being lowered on him. It would appear that it was better to swallow the loss of his daughter to a man he disliked, than losing his position and name in the community. There were few of us there, and we went for a meal afterwards. I tried to make some conversation with Ewing, but he was monosyllabic in his replies. Ally noticed and during the coffee stage decided to have her say. She rapped a spoon against a glass to get everyone's attention.

"I have just married the man I love. The man whose child I carry with great happiness. He is everything a girl could ask for, kind, generous, loving, but most importantly caring. I am so happy, and I wish that all my family could be happy for me." She looked pointedly at her father. "Jack and I are one. Slight Jack and you slight me. If he doesn't wish to see someone because of their attitude to him, then I will not see that person either. That's the way it will be. We come as a couple not divisible." Ewing had no doubt that tirade was aimed at him. Sheila looked daggers at him. We would just have to wait to see how he reacted. He did pay for the meal though.

Ally and I went to Jersey for a week, as a kind of honeymoon, promising each other that we could would make up later with a month long trip to Australia, somewhere we both had always wanted to visit. Ally assured me when we got into our suite that making love would not harm the baby in any way. With that she waltzed around the room leaving various items of her clothing draped over whatever happened to be near as she took them off. She then posed naked on the bed. "Jack, you have too many clothes on. Get naked Husband. Your wife needs you," We both loved hearing those words. She pointed with her finger and opened her legs. "Here! " We made love, slowly and deliciously. Afterwards I was lying with my head on her stomach. I turned slightly and kissed her belly.

"Grow strong little one." I whispered. "I love you already."

"Jack!" Ally's eyes glistened and smiled happily. "I always knew you would love her. You're that kind of man."

"Her? It may be a He." I reminded Ally.

"No, my Darling, It's a she. Trust me, a woman knows these things. Any way they say a man proves himself when he sires a daughter. I know you have proved yourself."

Six months later our daughter was born. Ally and I had long discussions about names. I wanted to call her Sheila after her mum, Ally wanted Jacqueline, the nearest she could get to my name. Guess what? I agreed to Jacqueline. Ally convinced me in bed one night, with a virtuoso performance with her mouth, playing a concerto on my cock. Yes, she was holding my balls in her hand at the time. I didn't dare disagree. We both knew that Jacqueline would grow up being called Jackie.

A couple of months had gone by when my suspicions were again aroused. I was getting the impression that Ally and Libby were conspiring together. I didn't get angry, despite the jest in which I had threatened Ally some time ago. It pleased me that Libby and Ally were getting close, and any way they showed me a great deal of love and affection. But I suspected I was being softened up for something. It came to a head one Sunday, when Libby turned up, just before lunch. Ally seemed to have expected her as she had already laid the table for three. I had cooked that day, and was glad that I had prepared a roast shoulder of Pork, so there was plenty. This left Ally free to be the good mother, which she was. She put Jacqueline down just before Lunch and we sat down. Both Ally and Libby seemed to be suppressing some excitement.

"OK, you two. What's going on?" I decided to challenge them.

Ally looked at me innocently. She was good at that. "Why should anything be going on?" Libby was trying to keep a straight face. I put her under pressure; she would crack faster than Ally.

"Libby! You appear to be hiding something. Now if this is a secret for the two of you, from which I am excluded, you can finish your meal, get back in your car and take your step mother with you. Perhaps both of you can remember what I said some months ago about your conspiring together." I tried, unsuccessfully to sound angry. Ally sighed.

"Go and get it, Lib. Before he throws the baby out with the bath water." Libby ran out to her car, and returned carrying a flat parcel about twenty inches by fourteen. She gave it to me.

"For you, Dad." Then Ally added some words.

"For making both of us so happy." I tore the paper off. Inside there was a framed picture. It was Ally and Libby recreating the pose I had admired so much before, they were nude as before, but this time smiling at the camera and with an addition, Jacqueline. They held her between them, Jacqueline's mouth being very close to Ally's nipple instinctively searching for her mother's milk. The photo had been mounted before being placed in the silver frame. On the mounting below the photo they had printed.

Jack's three Girls.

The End

Here is a sample from another story you may enjoy:

ABBY
CITY GIRL IN THE COUNTRY
EROTIC ROMANCE

KERRY JAMES

Abby had little difficulty in getting to this point, on the B3227 from Taunton heading towards South Molton, and guessed that somewhere on this road she should see a sign indicating her turn. Yet as she drove further and further into Devon she became uneasy that no such sign had revealed itself. Navigation became more of a problem as she drove deeper into the countryside, signposts, when you could find them; indicated a destination which then received no further mention at all upon succeeding signs. High banks on either side of the road meant that she had little clue as to where she was, the only point of reference was the ribbon of road unwinding ceaselessly and vanishing under the bonnet of her car and the occasional signs for some oddly named village or hamlet. As she passed through villages such as Wiveliscombe and Bampton, she wondered if she had gone wrong, and seeing the sign that said South Molton was just five miles farther on, decided that indeed she had gone wrong. Swearing mildly under her breath, Abby was giving thought to turning round and retracing her path.

Suddenly, she caught that breath; there was the sign. Leaning gently against the high banks that enclosed the road with a vigorous growth of Ivy as camouflage, she would have missed it had she not been driving slowly looking for a place to turn. It was a peculiar sensation, and her heart was beating furiously as she made the turn. A name that had previously existed only in hearsay and on a map was now a fact. Her mother had mentioned the name a few times without thinking, but would not be pressed on its significance. When her mother had died, Abby was nineteen, there was no reference at all to the name in her personal effects, which were few, there was no birth certificate, and the only official document she could find was an out of date passport, giving the birth area as South Molton. Abby's history consisted of just her mother's death certificates, and her own birth certificate. Abby now realised that she could have obtained a copy of her mother's birth certificate, but as is the way of things she had not thought logically at the time. She would repair this oversight as soon as possible. She wondered why her mum had a passport, as she had never travelled abroad.

Combe Linney, as Abby spelt it, was not even marked on her road map, and she had to resort to the Ordinance Survey to discover the location; again there was no place spelt Linney, but there was a Combe

Lyney, near South Molton, and she assumed that this had to be the place. Its sum total consisted of two black oblongs, and a round dot with a cross on top, presumably indicating a church. There were no A or B roads that ventured anywhere near the place. If this wasn't the back of beyond, then it was pretty close to it.

The mystery could not be investigated immediately as Abby had after her mother's death, to consider the business of life, a job, somewhere to live. Her mother had left her little, but a stubborn trait that helped Abby survive the numerous jobs she took in the financial and insurance trade; making tea and coffee for surly men and women who viewed her simply as the office gofer.; They would have been surprised if they had known that Abby did not merely put their drinks in front of them, but closely studied what they were doing. They didn't know because Abby was invisible, unimportant, not even missed when she left to go to a better job, using all she had learned to pack her C.V. She was twenty-five when she started in the city as a proprietary equity trader, the years of watching and learning placed her in good stead. She would not say that she was a brilliant trader, there were many more that could turn sixpences into sovereigns at the drop of a hat, but she was intuitive, and with no family to call upon her time, was content to work all hours to achieve her goal. In a business where employers counted the hours almost as important as the success, she was regarded highly.

To purchase this book, look for **Abby: City Girl in the Country**.

BBW
PLUS TWO

THE CRUISE SERIES, BOOK 2

JESSICA JOHANNSEN

Theresa didn't even bother with a greeting, just launched right into the questions.

"So, did you get laid or what?" Theresa asked, a big grin on her face.

"Good morning to you, too," Belinda said. She couldn't help but smile; her friend had a one-track mind.

"No, seriously," Theresa pressed. Theresa was like a bloodhound on the scent. "Did you get laid?"

"Yes!" Belinda squealed like a schoolgirl, unable to contain herself any longer. She sat up in bed, the blankets still around her. Though she'd once shared this bed with her husband, the bed was still hers and hers alone today. Right now, she was happy about that. Pressing the phone to her ear, she dished all her juicy gossip.

"He is amazing!"

"He?" Theresa asked, her enthusiasm waning. "You mean you only slept with one guy?"

"Because he was amazing," Belinda corrected her. "I spent the whole week in bed with him. I could hardly walk!"

Belinda didn't know why Theresa compelled her to spill things that she would otherwise never tell.

"That's more like it!" her friend whooped.

Theresa would allow her only the one lover as long as there were other, more lurid details.

"So, spill! Was he gorgeous?"

Belinda found herself humming and smiling when she thought about the intimate details of her time with Michael.

"God, yes. He's tall, handsome, gorgeous smile, perfect ass. He's in great shape, and he is so sweet." She could have gone on, but Theresa interrupted.

"What about his dick?"

Belinda blushed; her best friend had always been direct.

Belinda closed her eyes and remembered with relish and a contented sigh that particular part of her lover.

"It's perfect."

"And he knows how to use it?" Her friend was determined to hear the play by play, but Belinda thought that some things were best treasured in secret.

"I've never had so many orgasms," was all she would admit. As far as she was concerned, the subject was closed.

Theresa whistled in the phone.

"Damn girl, good for you," she said. She barely missed a beat. "So what are you doing about Stanley?"

This sigh was not so contented.

"Oh, Theresa, I don't know."

In Belinda's mind, the best week of her life had ended with a question mark rather than an exclamation mark. It was all because her smug bastard of a husband had been waiting on the dock for her.

"Supposedly, he broke up with Carly. He seems to think that makes it all better."

She couldn't wait to hear Theresa rip him a new one.

"Jesus! So now you should just take him back? Now that he's had his fun, that's what he thinks?" Theresa clicked her tongue. "I hope you told him to go to hell."

Belinda's stomach churned. She didn't want to answer, but there was no way to avoid Theresa's blunt question.

"Not exactly."

"What does that mean?" Theresa barked. "No, Belinda. Please tell me that you did not fuck him!"

"Of course not! Although he sure wanted to," Belinda replied.

"And you didn't kick him out?"

Theresa was an expert at playing the game so Belinda knew she should pay attention.

"Well, but we're not back together…" Belinda was justifying her actions, though she didn't know why she needed to. "I'm still seeing Michael."

She paused to give Theresa hope that there would be more men to discuss in the future as well.

"Michael, and anyone else I want to go out with."

Theresa was silent for a moment, as if weighing the choices.

"OK, I guess it's alright as long as you aren't taking him back," she laughed. "And you can still see other people. So when are you seeing Michael again?"

Belinda lay back, her head on the pillow, her eyes half glazed over with heat.

"Tonight. I can't wait."

"That's better," her friend cooed. Theresa was happier now, knowing that Belinda was playing the field. "Where are you meeting? Can you bring him to your house?"

Belinda gasped, giggled, and raised her hand to her mouth.

"I never even thought of that." It made her heart race though when she thought about it. "I was going to meet him at a hotel, but I guess I could bring him here, right?"

If you like this sample, look for **BBW Plus Two - The Cruise Series, Book 2 by Jessica Johannsen**.

Also by this Author:

Abby: City Girl in the Country

From the Author

If you enjoyed any of my books then please share the love and click like on my books in Amazon.

If you write me a review and send me an email I will send you a free book, or many.
(Just know that these emails are filtered by my publisher.)

Good news is always welcome.

One Last Thing, For Kindle Readers...

When you turn the page, Kindle will give you the opportunity to rate this book and share your thoughts on Facebook and Twitter. If you enjoyed my writings, would you please take a few seconds to let your friends know about it? Because... when they enjoy they will be grateful to you and so will I.

Thank You!

Kerry James
kerry_james@awesomeauthors.org

www.ingramcontent.com/pod-product-compliance
Lightning Source LLC
Chambersburg PA
CBHW071332130626
46556CB00004B/1871